The World Above 2 New Frontier:
By Benjamin Gorry

Author: Benjamin Gorry

Title: The World Above 2 New Frontier

Subject: Teen+ Story

Other titles:
   The Curse of the Slimy Green Monster 2013
   The World Above 2016

Cover design: Natasja Hellenthal
Production: ACS Publishing: +61 437 889 400
Year: 2018
ISBN: 978-0-9946173-1-6

Acknowledgements

Ben would like to thank the following for their assistance in putting this book together:

My parents Russell and Corinne for all their help and support,
My grandma Beryl Gorry for proof reading
Kathie Thomas from ACS Publishing for publishing and help with marketing
Adam Koya for providing constructive feedback, and
Nick Sowerbutts, for providing encouragement and discussions about the book.

The World Above
New Frontier
Prologue

"Run! Run away!"
As I shouted that, I grabbed my friend Kate and pulled her along to get away from the spinning water. Trails of water were floating out of every house and were combining into some kind of twister shooting all of it into the sky. As I felt a breeze flow through me, we managed to outrun the twister. When we escaped, all around us were trails of water floating mid-air everywhere. Pools, tanks, sinks, and even sewage had a trail of water leaving each of those things and spinning into three spots in the area.

As this was happening, I turned back to see if the spinning water was close by, when a floating trail of water splashed into me. Then as I ran out of it, the water that was soaked into my clothes was pulling me and a bunch of other people into the spinning water. Kate tried to pull me away until we saw another twister appearing near us, twisting water into the sky. Then before we realised it, we ended up pulled into the twister.

I looked around inside the twister and saw things like goldfish and other sea life that followed the water into the sky, but soon I couldn't see much as water continued to splash my face after every breath. Then as I felt a little faint from the lack of air, I let go of Kate's hand, not being able to grab it again. I waved my arms around trying to find her until I saw a figure in the distance collapse. Then as the water was almost lifting me, I blacked out and fell to the ground.

"Michaela wake up. Wake up Michaela."
I tried to recognise that Kate was yelling this at me so I decided to open my eyes and get up. I looked around the place and saw that the streets were covered in a crowd of people inspecting the area.

"How long was I out for?" I asked Kate.
"Not sure. I only just got up as well," said Kate.
Then as I was talking with her, I started to notice that the ground seemed to be shaking. Then Kate appeared to have a look of confusion on her face. I looked along the road and noticed cracks appearing everywhere.

I also started hearing screams from the distance. As I stood up, I noticed that houses started to fall apart and crumble into the ground. That's when I yelled at Kate to run. We saw everyone trying to get away from something. As we turned around, we started to run in the same direction as everyone else when I noticed more cracks appearing in the road. Then chunks of the road popped out of the ground around me while the screams of people dying flooded my ears. Soon I got tired and slowed down. Until Kate stopped and encouraged me to keep going.

When I looked to the side, I saw houses collapse as the ground started to tilt. Then Kate and I fell over. Kate tried to stand up again, but fell over once more, causing her to start sliding down the road towards a massive hole spreading towards her. People around me were tripping up on the cracks in the roads and were falling into the massive hole right behind us. As the ground tilted steeper, I tried to climb up the road as Kate followed from behind. When I made it to the top, spinning circles appeared around the two of us, and as more spinning circles appeared around us, a bright light emerged.

I wasn't sure why there was a bright light in front us, but then I saw a hand appear from the light and reach for me. Then another hand appeared reaching for Kate. The ground we were laying on was crumbling around the two of us and we had no choice. We grabbed the hands as the ground disappeared from under us, but for some reason, we weren't falling.
We were floating above the giant hole and saw many people falling into it, disappearing into the dust below with rocks falling from the sides. Then before we could see any more of it, we got pulled into the light and disappeared into it. All I could see was blurred colours and spinning circles when I blacked out again.

I opened my eyes and all I saw was people running around me, and that's when I noticed Kate next to me as well. We stood up wondering what happened to us when we noticed a car in front with two guys and some crazy cat running all over the place. Then Kate cut in front of me, grabbed my arm and pulled me to the car.
"We'll try to climb into the car so we can get driven off," yelled Kate.
"No! We'll run out of time, we need to keep running," I yelled back.
"We have to at least try or else we'll fall backward into the hole again," yelled Kate.
Kate immediately ran towards the car, but as she got near it, someone got to it first, opened the door and got in. We hadn't run past the car, so we ran around it and as we got near the other car door, someone else opened it and climbed inside it.

Frustrated Kate tried to shake the car to get the guy's attention, but it was just tiring. The guys in the car didn't even notice it since everyone around the car was hitting and shaking it. Kate then got frustrated and opened the door, when another guy got pushed in front of her and fell into the car, pulling the door shut. The doors had been locked after that. Then as the number of people running around them was shortening, Kate and I tried to climb the car from behind. The car wasn't starting up for some reason, but when they noticed that basically everyone was gone. The trench wasn't really spreading any more.

I was prepared to just wait it out on top of the car with Kate and go to the right until I looked forward and noticed a giant boat-shaped object in front of us further away. Then because the car wasn't moving, everyone ran out of the car and headed towards the boat. As they were running, I motioned Kate to jump off the car and head in the other direction. When we were jumping off, a couple of the guys turned back and saw us jump off the car, and continued on their run to the boat.

The guys were running off with a cat following behind them, when Kate and I realised the trench had stopped spreading just before it reached the car. We were running off when we noticed that the car looked a little battered, but seemed drivable. I told Kate that we should head back to the car, even though part of it was in the ground.

The guys were arguing about something and for some reason, they ended up deciding to sit on an anchor that had just landed. Kate walked in front of me as we headed closer to the car, when we noticed the wheels sink into the ground a little more.

Kate slowly opened up the door and climbed inside as I followed from behind. The guys weren't even paying attention to the car anymore as they were just trying to start some kind of small talk. Some smaller cracks were spreading around the car as it started to roll back a little when I finally climbed inside and shut the door.

"Kate start up the car and let's go!" I whispered.

"Michaela, I'm trying, but the cars not starting for some reason," stammered Kate.

Then as parts of the ground around the car started to crumble into the trench, Kate turned the key the best she could for a final try while I was trying to edge her on to hurry up. Then as the ground behind the car crumbled into the trench, the car started up, just as the back wheels were hanging over the edge of the trench.

Kate immediately pushed down on the accelerator to start making the front wheels drive forward, just as the car was falling backwards. The front wheels drove them out of the ground as the trench was spreading under them very slowly. The back wheels were on the ground again as they started to drive away from the guys and the trench.

I wasn't sure if the guys even realised we'd taken the car. They probably figured it had fallen into the trench as we drove off.

I got out my phone to call my parents and realised I had no internet connection. Confused, I told Kate about it and she got out her phone to check her internet connection, only to realise that it wasn't working either.

I wasn't sure where we were going and neither did Kate. All we knew was that we were going somewhere away from the giant hole that resembled a trench, and even though we probably weren't going to make it, we would try our best to work out what had happened to the world, and how we could fix it.

But there was still one thing on my mind, "Why were the guys sitting on the giant anchor?"

The World Above
New Frontier
Chapter 1
Within the Vortex

"Where am I? How did I get here?" All I could see around me was darkness. Nothing but darkness. I couldn't even see myself. Then as darkness surrounded me, a light appeared. I tried to reach out for it, but it was too far away. Then I saw some spinning circles around me. I wasn't sure what the spinning circles represented, or why they were here, but then more of them appeared, and I started to disappear.

I started to get sleepy as I shut my eyes, when I was spun in the circles with the light growing bigger and brighter. Then as the light started to spread around me, I was able to see myself again, but I couldn't believe what I could see. I didn't have a tail anymore. And I had lost all of my fur. My whiskers were gone and my paws were hands! I couldn't even recognise myself anymore. I, Adam, had become human.

I always thought I had imagined it, but it was true. Then as the light flew through me, it continued to pull me into it. My arms were twisting in circles and my legs had become as rubbery as spaghetti. Then my head sank into my body as my arms and legs disappeared. Then my body got pulled into the light and I vanished.

I opened my eyes wondering where I was. Then I realised I was in a vortex. Colourful circles spun around me as I fell through it, and when I looked around, I saw outlines of three people around me. Then the outlines became shadows. Then they became people in the same position as me. I didn't know who they were or what they were doing here so I just figured that they were going through the same thing as me.

I decided to just wait for the vortex to end until I saw what was happening to the others. They were beginning to vanish. Their fingers had started to vanish and the same thing was happening to me so I needed to escape. My feet had vanished so I tried to push myself into the side of the vortex, thinking it would send me back. I stuck my arm into it and felt a huge surge of pain go through my arm and noticed the other people start to stare at me.

I realised that this was a bad idea, but I couldn't pull my arm out. As my legs fell through it, my other arm was falling into it as well. Then when I looked up, I noticed the other guys didn't actually look human. They were blue ghostly beings with see-through plasma like stuff surrounding their bones. Then as one of the blue beings opened its mouth, it started to reach out its wrist for me to grab until I completely fell out of the vortex.

All I saw around me was darkness again. Except above me, there was a colourful cylinder looking thing that I was drifting away from. As I drifted away from it, I started to fade away and my fingers were becoming see-through. Then a ghostly face appeared in front of me. It was trying to talk to me, but I couldn't understand a thing it was saying as it was just mumbling and talking gibberish. Then I noticed it begin to seem worried as it started to float above me and moved back into the vortex.

I figured something was wrong so I tried to grab it, until I realised it was intangible. My feet had faded away and so had my fingers. I had to get back into the vortex or else I would fade away in the darkness. Then as I looked up once more, I noticed the spirit float back into the vortex. I thought I was doomed as there was no way back up until I noticed one of the blue beings stick its face out of the vortex.

Then as the creature stared at me, it opened its mouth and reached a hand through the vortex to reach for my wrist. I realised that it might be on my side so I stretched my arm up to it, but because my legs were furthest away they were already gone and so was part of my body. Then the creature came out of the vortex to reach for me.

I stretched my arm as far as I could and soon the skeleton grabbed my arm and tried to pull me back into the vortex. Then the skeleton screamed in pain as it was getting pulled back into the vortex while my legs, hands, and fingers were reappearing again. As my head managed to push through the vortex, I tried to ignore the pain.
I looked around inside the vortex and I saw one of the Blue Beings fall apart and disappear into the exit. The one that pulled me into the vortex waved at me as it also fell apart and disappeared into the exit. I looked at my hands and realised that they had vanished and so had my arms. Then I saw the other one holding the spirit in place.

The spirit then tried to talk to me as it tried to escape, but all I could hear was, "You're looped, you're looped, you're looped. Then the blue being threw the spirit back into me as it vanished into the vortex. I wasn't sure what was thrown into me and I didn't want to fall out of the vortex again so I let myself vanish into the end of it.

I had become a bunch of small pieces flying through the vortex as I disappeared into the light. Once again, darkness surrounded me as flashing lights soon appeared. Then green vines appeared around me and wrapped around both my wrists and legs. The vines squeezed harder as they started to spread up my arms. The vines had stretched up to my neck and seemed to strangle me, and that was when I saw two bright red eyes appear in front with a toothy grin underneath. Then the mouth opened up and ate me whole.

I thought I was dead, until I realised I could still see things. A bunch of numbers appeared around me in a circle, and then I realised it was becoming a giant clock. The hands of the clock started to spin in circles spinning faster and faster. Suddenly a hole appeared in the middle of the clock and I started to get pulled into it. As I got pulled into it, I saw clocks spinning around me, then years appeared in front of me until I vanished and ended up somewhere else.

I was drifting through the vortex when I saw an image of a person's face appear in front, when I realised it was an image of me. It slowly started to change though, and the face slowly grew whiskers and pointy ears as the image of my face became a cat face. Then all of the images disappeared around me as I heard loud donging sounds from the clocks that surrounded me and I blacked out again. Then as I blinked, flashing lights appeared around me and I realised I had woken up.

I was back in the bathroom where I had collapsed before. I was sweating all over with my heart pumping hard.

"It was just a dream,"

"Just a creepy made-up dream."

Then as I tried to go back to sleep a ghostly voice appeared inside my head.

"Was it a dream?"

"Or was it a vision of the future?"

I was known to have visions occasionally, but they never lasted that long before, and usually they were just faint images, so how could any of that ever happen to me.

It just wasn't possible.

The World Above
New Frontier
Chapter 2
Waking Up

Beep, Beep, Beep, Beep. "Wake up Lily," called her dad. "Ah seriously? Already? Fine! I better get up." I reached across my bed and stopped my alarm. Then as I rolled over, I slowly stood out of bed and started to get ready to leave. I walked out of my bedroom, kicked off my socks and undressed myself to have a shower. I turned on the hot air tap and cold air appeared around me so I quickly stood out of the shower as the air was too cold. And as the air heated up, I washed myself in it.

About ten minutes later, I left the shower and started to get dressed. I saw a good pair of pants on the ground, but it was inside out. As I reached in and fixed up the two legs, I also fixed up the tail leg. Then as I put on my pants, I flattened my back fin as I put on my t-shirt and jumper. Soon I put on my socks and noticed how dry my feet were, so I wrapped my feet in the towel to make my feet moister, then put my socks on.

I walked into the kitchen where I opened up the food cupboard to see what to have for breakfast. I had a choice of different types of cereals such as Weed-Brits, Plank Flakes (Plankton Flakes), KKPops (Krill Krill Pops) or Oats. I wasn't sure what to grab but I decided to grab the packet of KK Pops to eat. I looked inside the fridge for some milk and I realised it was nearly finished. I poured the rest of the milk in my bowl and threw the container in the bin.

I sat down at the dining table and as I was about to eat some of my breakfast, I remembered my pet humans. They were probably hungry. I went to grab the human food and I tapped a little extra into the tank for the new humans. I've always been interested in what it's like to have food fall from the sky, but I guess I'll never really know. I wonder what those humans do all day in that tank, especially with that ten-second-memory problem. I always enjoy watching the humans running out of their house to grab that food. I don't know how they can eat that stuff though. It's quite slimy and it just falls apart.

"Honey it's time to go now," shouted Dad. I had just finished my breakfast when he called that out and immediately ran back to my room to grab a jacket. This was because it was usually really cold early in the morning out in the ocean. I understand why my dad wants to go humaning this early. I think it's got something to do with the low tide or something. As I headed out the door, I put on my shoes and jumped into the sea carcumber since humaning with Dad was usually exciting.

I've always wanted to ride in the humaning boat on the way to the pier, but then I think about how cold it would be on the way there and how my dad would always say no to me. I jumped into the sea carcumber as dad started the drive to the pier. I was going on another humaning trip and I was hoping to catch a lot of humans, from salesman to fatheads. I'll be happy with whatever I catch, and even though I'm keeping the other ones safe, I'm still hoping to catch dinner.

The World Above
New Frontier
Chapter 3
Pet Humans

Meanwhile in the human tank...

"Hey, they're feeding us early this time." As the burgers fell from the sky, the giant fish walked away. Regen and Frazer ran out of the house with Nick and John following behind him. Scott stumbled from behind half asleep as he just wanted to grab some food and go back to bed. As they were running around to catch the burgers from the sky, John and Bruce seemed to be fighting over the burgers. Regen remembered the newcomers and decided to go back inside to wake them up. Teresa only grabbed one burger as she wasn't that hungry and knew that the others would also need food as they were much bigger than them.

Ben started to wake up as he noticed some grease on the windows. He looked outside and saw that some kind of food was falling from the sky. Then Regen smashed through the door telling them to get up and have something to eat. Seth and Tom decided to follow Regen outside to check out the breakfast while Ben went to check on Adam.

As Seth and Tom exited the house, they noticed that there was a bunch of burgers scattered all over the ground, but not falling apart, they decided to pick up a burger when Bruce walked over and yelled, "That better be the only burger you need you, Giants!"

Seth and Tom decided to just walk off with their burger and let the others have their breakfast. They were both visitors in their home so they didn't argue back at Bruce.

Ben walked to the bathroom where Adam was to make sure he was okay, and as he opened the door, he noticed that Adam had slept in the bath with the towel as a blanket. Ben went back to get a pair of pants and a T-shirt and laid them on him. Adams face was bright red and sweating while shivering at the same time.

Ben wasn't sure what had happened to Adam but also decided to let him rest. Adam was Ben's ordinary house pet that night until he changed from a cat to a human. The whole idea of Adam being a person was weird, but Ben decided to leave him and see what was outside. He needed Adam to rest, so he'd be okay for the day.

Ben was walking out of the room when blue spinning circles were appearing and a bright blue light formed in front of him. As Ben looked into the light, a person emerged from it saying, "Hey, it's me again, Beth. I just thought I should see you now, in case you forgot me."

Startled, Ben stood backwards as he said, "Yep, I do remember you. How are you doing that? You still haven't told me yet?"
"Don't worry about it, you'll work it out eventually, but for now, I'm just here in case you may need help, in which I should warn you. You should plan your escape soon and get out of here. I can't say why yet, but you need to get out."
"Okay then, but I still don't really know who you are. Have we met before?"

"No, not yet. You haven't met me yet, and I haven't either. You'll know all about that soon, but for now, I think I have to leave so, see ya later."

As Beth and the blue light vanished, Ben was left there wondering who she was, but also knew that she had been right about things in the past so he left the house to see the others. He thought it may be a better idea to not tell anyone about Beth for a while since she would be difficult to explain.

As Ben left the bathroom, Adam slowly opened his eyes and saw the clothes next to him. He was breathing heavily and tried to stand up. He picked up the clothes not really knowing what to do with them as he didn't need clothes as a cat. Then when he put on his clothes, he started to try and walk, but fell over straight away. He knew it would take him awhile to walk so he had to practise now.

Ben picked up a burger off the ground, noticing that it hadn't fallen apart or gotten muck on it. Then he noticed a size difference between him and the original human tank members. He and the others were a little bigger than the ones in the human tank. As Ben looked around, he noticed that he and the others would soon get caught and served to the table so they had to escape.

Ben ran over to Tom and asked if he could blast his way out of the tank, but Tom just replied with "I've talked about it with Seth and he said that it probably wasn't a good idea to destroy this place as it was home to the others, and that he wanted to save up his missiles a bit."

Adam was practising walking around in circles to strengthen his legs when an image started to appear in his head. All the image had was darkness, until two glowing red eyes emerged from the darkness. Then a grinning mouth also appeared and as it opened its mouth, it spoke two words over and over again, "You're looped, you're looped, you're looped."
Then the image faded away with Adam being more confused about the two words than how he turned human. Why was it all happening to him? Then he ran out of the bathroom and staggered through the hallway and fell over many times. He realised he still needed some more walking practice.

As Josh was eating his burger, he looked out the window through the human tank and noticed that it was raining outside, although the rain wasn't water, it was air. He told Rusheel about this and agreed that it was weird, but it also meant that now was a great time to leave so they could collect more air to breathe in. As they ran to Seth and Tom, they noticed Rusheel walking out of the house holding Adam up to make sure he didn't fall. Then he also noticed Bailey following after them looking for breakfast.

Rusheel managed to help Adam over to Seth, Josh, Harry, and Ben, knowing that they needed to find a way out of there. Tom pulled Bailey away for a moment to talk to him about something. Then when Bailey agreed to Tom's question, he said, "Okay, but they better be good ones then."
After that, they walked back to the others. Jared and Jacob were having a sleep-in and weren't noticing what was going on outside. Jacob started to slowly wake up, thinking that everything that had happened to them was a dream, but then he saw Jared and realised it wasn't. He decided to leave the room, go outside and leave Jared to sleep.

Jacob was outside when he noticed Frazer talking to John. Jacob decided to see what they were talking about so he ran over to them. Frazer and John turned to Jacob as Jacob asked, "Hey, just wondering if I could hang out with you guys for a bit." Jacob stood with Frazer and John for a while. Then Frazer answered him with "Sure, you can hang with us…hey you want to be part of our group?"
"Sure," answered Jacob.

Then as Frazer talked to Jacob, John just stood near them and stayed quiet as he listened to them talk. He and Frazer knew that it would be cool to have a giant person with them to help around the place. When Frazer was done talking to Jacob, he agreed to it since the tank would provide a healthy life for him. Then as Frazer and John walked over to the others, Frazer got Jacob to go back to his group so that there wasn't any suspicion of him staying back.

Scott decided he was ready to fully get up so he walked outside to where the others were. Regen, Frazer, Nick, Teresa, John, Scott and Bruce decided to sit in a group and talk about what had happened that night. They were still confused about what the War was and who was trying to pull them into the light. Then they saw the others having their own conversation and noticed that one of the others had a robot arm like the one that tried to pull them into the light.

Then they all turned to Bruce, and Nick asked, "Actually where were you Bruce? You didn't even try to help us." "What are you talking about, you guys know that I'm a deep sleeper so I probably just didn't hear you guys. Anyway, why didn't the new-comers help you guys either?" yelled Bruce.

"I don't know why they didn't help us and why Tom has the same robot arm as the one that came out of the light, but we have to work it out."

"Maybe they came to us because they wanted to save us. What if it is the others, but it's them from the future. What if the new-comers are time travellers?" said Regen.

"Don't be stupid Regen that's impossible," said Bruce.

While they were talking, the new-comers were talking about an escape plan. They had ideas of blasting their way out, but they didn't want to destroy the others home. After arguing about how they'd escape, Ben had an idea, "What if we climbed out using the house."

Rusheel decided to run back into the house to wake up Jared so everyone worked out the plan and were prepared to escape.

The World Above
New Frontier
Chapter 4
The Tank Escape

As Regen and the others were chatting, Teresa noticed the new-comers running into the house. Then before they knew it, Frazer followed behind them. Regen and the others wanted to know where Frazer and the new-comers were going so they followed them into the house. Tom was at the top of the house, stretched his hand to the side of the bowl and jumped off. The robot arm pulled him to the top and as he let go, he stretched back to the house so the others could walk across and yelled, "Hey guys, do ya need a hand."

As Tom waited, he noticed Bailey wryly laugh as everyone else groaned from what Tom had said. Then Tom decided to look over his shoulder and saw out of place patches of air all over the table to help everyone walk around a little better.

Seth looked out the window and noticed that it was raining a lot harder than before. Then he remembered the fish saying that they were going on a humaning trip, and that's when he realised that they needed to escape soon before it was too late. Josh was first to walk across as Seth was edging them all to hurry up. When Josh reached the tip of the bowl, Jared walked across after him. Josh pulled the air mask out of his pocket and placed it on his face as he slid down the bowl. Then as Jared slid down, Rusheel and Adam were next as they walked across the arm and slid down the bowl.

Rusheel got up and walked across the table while Adam followed behind him without needing an air mask. Then as everyone followed over the bowl, they grabbed an air mask off Tom on the way. Rusheel and Adam were looking down the table, wondering if they could survive the fall, when they noticed Jared and Josh climbing down one of the chairs.

Then as Seth and Harry followed down the chair, Adam decided to jump off the table and land on his feet. Rusheel realised that even though Adam was once a cat and had some kind of paranormal power, he thought that maybe he could jump too, and that was when he saw a doorknob turn on the front door.

Bailey had fully made it across when Ben started walking across the arm as well. Then when Ben made it across, Tom said, "Look at me single 'handily help everyone out."
"Ha, nice one Tom!" yelled Bailey.
Confused, Ben figured Bailey thought everything was funny to him so he said to Tom, "Yeah, keep up the good work bro." The original human tank members were curious about what was going on when Regen decided to join them and walk across as well. Everyone thought he was crazy for going with them when Nick followed behind him as well. Jacob started to follow onto the arm when everyone waiting behind thought the others were crazy for wanting to escape. Then Frazer pushed in front and started to lift Tom's fingers from the house.

Ben started to slide down the bowl when Tom realised what Frazer was doing and yelled, "Hey, what are you doing."
"I'll tell you what I'm doing. I'm saving everyone's lives by stopping them from leaving home."

"Frazer stop, just let us cross," yelled Nick as Regen was on the edge of the bowl.

"No. I've lost too many people in the past. And none of us want to lose you guys too. Why are you even leaving?"

"Because it's boring in here, and we want to explore and escape this unknown world. You should come and join us so that you'll know it's safe."

"No, it's too dangerous out there, and I won't let you guys leave because of it."

"Mhmm, then you can't decide my fate. I'll do whatever I want!"

Then just as Nick yelled that, he ran across Toms' arm and slid down the bowl with Regen. Jacob wasn't sure where he should go when Frazer released Toms' robot arm and made Jacob fall.

While Tom was struggling with his arm, he noticed from the corner of his eye that the fish walking around looked quite frustrated and annoyed. It didn't notice Tom and the others escaping as it walked into a different room. Jacob was hanging onto the arm when another fish walked through the door, also not noticing the humans. Jacob was sliding down the robot arm when Tom realised Jacob was going to detach the arm from his shoulder.

Tom knew that the robot arm didn't have the strength to pull Jacob up after having everyone walk across it. He had to stretch it back up and make Jacob fall to the ground. Tom immediately slid down the bowl as he turned back to see the others looking at him. Then he noticed the smaller fish walk over to them.

As soon as the fish saw Tom, it immediately yelled out for her dad to get up and check out the humans. He yelled, "Lily, you know that humans can't climb out of the human tank. They're just not smart enough. Remember their ten-second memory pro..." And that was when he saw the pet humans escaping across the dining table.

It was still pouring with air and while the others thought it might give them a chance to fill up their air masks, Seth knew that they couldn't use the air falling from the sky as that was probably fresh air. They could only have salt air for some strange reason. Jacob was hitting the glass bowl with his hands even though he knew it was pointless. Then Frazer walked up to Jacob and started to reassure him that what he did was a good thing. Jacob wasn't sure though, and neither were the others.

"Lily, go and block the door so the humans can't escape. They shouldn't be able to. But you never know," said the fish to his daughter. Lily immediately ran over to the door to hold it shut while watching the humans flop on the ground and constantly fall over. Adam stood around with everyone, wondering why they were falling all over the place. Then he ran over to Josh and Seth and helped them to their feet. Adam noticed that everyone's feet were sliding across the ground so he grabbed Seth's wrist and told him to grab Josh's.

Ben walked to the edge of the table with Regen next to him and noticed the giant fish reach for Ben. Then as Ben looked directly at the fish, he sensed that the fish were psychotic beings who felt joy from hurting them. He'd watched this fish try to kill him before, and he needed to get away before the fish caught him again.

Rusheel was still nearby and pulled out his guns. He was surprised that they were loaded with eight bullets but just decided to think he forgot they were there and shot the fish in the arm. Regen noticed Rusheel shooting the fish when Regen fell on his back and slipped off the table. He landed on a chair not far below with a cushion on it and slid off that too. Then Rusheel looked at his bullet count, realising he only had four bullets left.

Adam had Seth and Josh sliding behind him and as they were sliding to the door, Adam turned back, let go, and went back to help the others while Seth and Josh fell over onto the ground. The giant fish wasn't really hurt by the bullets, but it could still feel the pain and swiped Ben and Regen off the table and onto the chair. Tom saw this and as the fish turned to him, he switched his robot arm into a missile launcher. This made the fish back off a little. Then he turned it back to normal before he could fall and accidentally launch a missile by mistake. That's when he got an idea to help him walk better.

Regen was being protected by the shield as he jumped off the chair with Ben and hit the ground, thinking the shield protected them from the fall a little. Then as they stood up and walked to the others, they both made everyone around wonder how they were walking properly. Then when Ben explained it to them, he had an idea to enable everyone around to walk properly. He got Bailey to try and stand near him when Nick crawled over to see what was going on.

Tom enlarged his robot arm a little, shoved it into the table and made it lift him into the air, allowing the arm to walk for him. Although Lily wanted to keep the humans inside, she was also fascinated by how they were all helping each other up. Then she watched the human with the robot arm leap off the table and land on his metal hand. Tom noticed that people were struggling to stand and that's when he had an idea to help them. He created a little ledge for him to stand on, stretched his arm across the ground as a bit of path, and left the fingers on the end to move him around.

When Ben saw that a good group of people were around him, he deactivated the shield, touched Bailey, turned the shield back on, and watched as the shield spread around him, Bailey, Nick, and Regen. "For the shield to keep us protected, we have to stick together," said Ben.

And as everyone agreed to that, they started to run to the door. Tom managed to get Jared so they were able to stand properly on his robot arm and allowed them to travel to the door. Harry was attempting to stand by himself since he was told he'd be able to after he was merged with a plastic fish during the science experiment he participated in.

Then as Harry tried to stand up, he immediately slipped up and fell over. Tom was crawling by when this happened and offered Harry a ride. Although Harry wanted to be an independent explorer, he knew that he needed help so he climbed onto the robot arm and travelled with the others.

When Tom noticed Bailey nearby, he said, "I hope this helps you stand up for yourself later on."
Bailey heard it and decided to laugh a little while everyone else groaned at Tom once again. It seemed weird that Tom was trying to pull off a joke every so often since he'd never really done that before.

Adam noticed Rusheel falling over, and got Josh to grab Rusheel's hand. Then as Adam was running and allowing them to slide behind him, he was just amazed that they all didn't fall over.

The adult fish noticed how the humans separated into three groups and helped each other out. He was just amazed at how they were actually walking on their land because humans had never done that before. He still wanted to catch them though. He noticed they looked similar to the ones he caught the day before and still wanted something to eat that night. That's when it walked over to the humans with the glove and the filleting knife.

Ben's group made it to the door first while Adams group followed with Toms. They looked at the door and there wasn't a crack for them to escape through. And as the fish was about to reach them, Lily opened the door a little, letting all of them escape.
"Lily, why did you open it for them?" Asked her dad.
"My hand slipped, I'll just get out of the way," said Lily.
And as she walked off, she thought about what she did and was happy she did it. Any human skilled enough to stand and run deserved to escape, but they were on their own now.

The World Above
New Frontier
Chapter 5
The Open World

When Ben saw Lily open the door for them, part of him started to believe that they weren't psycho beings. Until the bigger fish continued to chase after them.

Although Toms way of travelling across the ground was slower, everyone managed to keep a good balance. While Ben's group was a bit faster, the shield was weakening as people slowed down or sped up.

Adams group was getting pulled along the ground and nearly falling over at times. Seth, Josh and Rusheel were trying to keep balanced. They all escaped through the door and managed to get down the stairs. Toms arm just stretched everyone down while Ben's group were jumping at the same time. Adams group however just fell over and slid down the stairs.

They all managed to get down and noticed a yard of long seaweed. As the fish followed them through the door and down the stairs, it suddenly thought that maybe he should have mowed the lawn the day before. The three groups ran in different directions through the seaweed.

The fish noticed that the humans were splitting up and went to chase the group in the middle. As Adam and the others were running, they started to feel the ground move under them, and that's when a head appeared out of the ground with hundreds of legs following behind it as Seth yelled, "Watch out for the Beach Worms!"

While Adam was pulling the others with his sudden strength and strong grip, he started to notice that his other hand was enlarging. Then he saw another Beach worm in front of him and spotted others around as well. The Beach worms were really fast and although they didn't really bite them, they were scratching their skin and covering their legs with bruises and scratches.

Then as they all started to slow down, Josh noticed that Adam wasn't scratched at all. Even when he was scratched, he would just heal instantly. Then before Adam knew it, a Beach worm burst from the ground heading for his head so he punched it away with his fist.

Adam let go of Josh's arm and that hand also became bigger and stronger. Although he wasn't sure why this was happening, he didn't really care. He just liked the idea of having some kind of superpower. And as the Beach worms were biting the others all over the ground, he attempted to jab them in the head with his fist, but they were too quick for him so he had another idea that he knew the others probably wouldn't enjoy. He held Josh and Seth in place in front of him while Rusheel was sitting behind him preparing to shoot the next one that appeared.

Tom was the slowest group of them all, but he was mainly surprised at how his arm was holding this weight. Then as he was brushing through the seaweed, he noticed loud footsteps behind him, and that's when Jared turned around and saw the fish behind, reaching down to grab them. The fish was waving his hand through the seaweed trying to catch one of the humans as he waved his hands through the seaweed to the left and missed, then waved to the right when he hit Tom in the head, and that's when Tom decided to get rid of this threat for good.

Tom yelled at everyone to get off, so Harry and Jared jumped off while slipping and falling over. Then as Tom stretched his hand back to normal size, he stood strongly on the ground, grew his hand into a massive fist, palmed the ground, and as the fish was about to grab him, propelled himself off the ground, lifted his fist into the air, and smashed it in the face with the robot fist.

Tom fell to the ground while slipping over and falling, but also making the fish fall backwards with a loud thud. He turned his arm back into a track for everyone to ride on and looked back to see that the fish was still down. Harry was still trying to stand up, and just as he was starting to walk, he lost balance and fell over when Tom landed. This caused him to accept that he needed more practice and continued to travel with Tom.

Ben and the others saw the fish fall over. They looked forward and saw a dirt hill in front of them and ran through it. Immediately as they ran through it, little critters crawled out of a hole. As they spread across the ground, Regen and Bailey got a few of them around their feet, but Nick on the other hand had them crawling all over his legs and biting him, making him fall over and break the shield.

The shield immediately fixed itself around everyone, but left Nick behind even as he was screaming for help. The spread of the critters grew too large amounts as they were smothering him. He tried to reach into his pockets to grab an air mask, but as he placed it on his face, he passed out, while the critters continued to bite him.

Ben and the others realised Nick wasn't there anymore and wanted to go back for him, but also noticed the spread of the amphipods. As the critters spread towards them, they started to climb over the shield. When they saw Nick's limp body on the ground, they figured he was dead and ran off to get out of the seaweed before they were next.

The plan was working for a while, even if Seth and Josh hated every moment of it. Adam had them in front of him and when the beach worms were crawling up their legs, Adam would crush their heads, while Rusheel sat behind shooting at what tried to bite from behind. After three were crushed, Josh and Seth noticed that their ankles had scratches everywhere and tears all over their pants. Then with one bullet remaining, Adam had a hunch that there was only one beach worm left and had a plan to pull it out of the ground to see what it really looked like.

The beach worm was being a real pain, and Adam would wait for it climb up either Seth or Josh's leg so he could grab it, but he would always miss or have it slip out of his grip. He was about to give up when Seth and Josh both agreed to help get it out as they didn't want their legs getting scratched anymore. The beach worm started to crawl up Josh's leg and slowly reach the waist as Adam went to grab its head slowly with two hands, and with the help of Josh and Seth, they managed to slowly grab its head to calm it, then fully grab it and pull the whole thing out of the ground as Rusheel stared in amazement at what they did.

The beach worm was thrown above their heads and as all the hundreds of little feet were rapidly moving around, Adam crushed its head, leaving it spooled on the ground. Then Rusheel noticed another beach worm head appear, and as it slithered away, Rusheel pulled out his gun and shot it right in the forehead, making it stop moving for good.

They weren't very sure if the beach worm had two heads or not and they decided not to question that beach worms were found at beaches and not lawns, so Adam decided to grab Rusheel as he grabbed Seth who also grabbed Josh. They started to run through the seaweed hoping to find a footpath so they would be free from the backyard.

The fish stood up again being very dizzy and confused since he wasn't sure what had hit him that hard. As he stood up, questioning a human's potential, he saw Nick's limp body on the ground covered by many little amphipods. The fish bent over to pick him up, while hoping that he wouldn't get attacked by the human again. The fish noticed that Nick wasn't moving and decided to bring him to the porch where Nick would rest headless on the chopping board.

Ben, Regen and Bailey felt pretty sorry for Nick as the fish carried him away. They didn't even really know who he was. Then as they brushed some seaweed away, they realised that walking was a lot easier now and that the shield wasn't being the thing keeping them balanced anymore. They looked at the ground and noticed that it had turned kind of pale. Then a smoke bomb landed on them. Everyone believed it to be a smoke bomb, but they also noticed lots of these were appearing from the sky along with the drops of air. Bailey realised that it was starting to hail, and the air rain was making it easier to walk because it was drying up the land.

While Tom, Jared and Harry were experiencing the dried up land as well, Adams group was concerned about what was happening to Adam more than the ground as they stayed behind him. Adam checked the bottom of his feet and noticed spikes pointing out of his shoes, and that his hands had also enlarged as he continued to breathe underwater perfectly without an air mask. Although Adam was wondering about the visions of the future and his power of not getting hurt, he did want to focus on his hands and feet. There was still no explanation for them or anything.

As the fish pushed the knife down on Nick's neck, the fish gave a sigh of relief as Nick's head came off and was most definitely dead. The fish even decided to skin him a little by cutting off his hands and feet as he deboned him to prepare for dinner. When the fish finished, he walked back inside and had a thought. If the humans in the tank now knew how to escape, they might try again. So the fish grabbed a bucket, walked over to the human tank, and decided to get rid of the problem.

"Dad, did you manage to catch them?" Asked Lily.
"I only managed to catch one Lil, but the humaning trip will have to wait until next week maybe since I need to rest my head about what I saw. I'm also going to dispose of your pet humans," said Lily's dad.
"Why?"

"I don't want to risk the others wanting to escape as well now that they know how to. Don't worry honey, I'll get some more from the pet store," said Lily's dad.

"Okay then," said Lily disappointedly as she walked to her room. She didn't want them killed, but she didn't want them escaping. She just let her father do what he wanted to do and remember the ones she let free.

The World Above
New Frontier
Chapter 6
Those that Stayed

"Frazer are you sure it was a good idea for us to stay here?" asked Jacob while everyone was just wandering around. "Of course it was. This was a brilliant idea. The others escaped so now the fish will go after them, catch them, and we'll be left here to use more oxygen, more room and more food," said Frazer.

The others were agreeing to this, but still thinking it was a bad idea when they saw a giant hand reach into the bowl, grab Frazer, pull him up and throw him into a bucket screaming for help. Then as Jacob and the others were running around the place, the fish knocked over the house. It collapsed and nearly landed on Scott. The fish was waving his hand around everywhere trying to grab them and managed to grip John and throw him into the bucket. Then he grabbed Teresa, Scott and everyone else. When Jacob saw a bike leaning nearby collapse on him, the fish grabbed him swiftly and threw him into the bucket.

Everyone had a bad feeling about where they were being taken and when the fish walked them outside, they knew that they were in trouble. The fish was at the chopping board under a roof to protect him from the rain. He grabbed Frazer and placed him on the board. Then everyone else and finally Jacob. They were all under water now so they couldn't breathe as the fish grabbed a knife. Jacob looked over and noticed the remains of Nick and realised in fear that this was the end and shut his eyes.

Jacob opened his eyes and looked over, just as the fish cut off Frazer's head. Then as he scraped Frazer away, he moved Bruce over, and the fish successfully sliced off his head as well. The fish then scraped him over and John was placed on the board, and as he was about to pass out, his head came off too. Then Scott was next, and as he was moved over, blue spinning circles appeared around him. Then just before the chop, Scott vanished. Confused, the fish quickly moved Teresa over. She passed out, just before the knife was to be pushed down on her neck, and vanished as well.

Jacob was now next and the fish was freaking out. He immediately tried to cut off his head when spinning circles appeared around Jacob, making him vanish into a blue light! Jacob looked around for everyone as he saw giant spinning circles surrounding him, and as he looked around, he noticed a blue creature absorb Teresa into its arm. Once she was absorbed, it turned to look at Jacob and Scott.

The fish was beginning to wonder if he was having eye problems and tried to imagine that they were never there. Then a green circle appeared around Nick's remains.

The green circle started to spin around Nick, turning faster and faster as his arms and feet joined back to his body again. His body was fixed with a full skeleton, and his head was stuck back on his body making him become alive again. And when he opened his eyes, he vanished into a blue light. The fish stood back stunned at what he just saw. Then he noticed another green circle appearing around Frazer and spinning circles around him.

As the fish wanted to stop this, he immediately grabbed Frazer's head in one hand, and his body in the other and tried to pull them away from each other, but the neck stretched through the fish's finger joining to the body. The fish felt a surge of pain as he noticed human skin appearing up his arm as Frazer was being absorbed into him. Freaking out, the fish started to shake his hand to get it off him, but it was also spreading through his body, his legs, his other arm and his head. And as a green light appeared around his body, he collapsed to the ground.

Nick woke up and as he opened his eyes, he looked around and saw giant spinning circles around him. The place he was in kind of looked like what you'd see in a vortex, but he wasn't quite sure where he was. Then as he looked around, the only beings near him were Jacob, Scott and three blue glowing creatures. Nick wasn't sure what they were, but then as one of them grabbed Jacobs head, he vanished into the blue creature's hand. Then Nick noticed another one reach for Scott and immediately got him absorbed in the creatures' hand as well.

As the third blue creature was floating towards Nick, he decided that he needed to escape from them and in a desperate struggle, made his hand fall into the side of the vortex. Then volts of pain appeared through his body making him scream for help. He noticed that he was getting pulled through the wall of the vortex. The strange blue creature grabbed him but also got electrocuted by Nick.

"We can't let him disappear into the void, he'll be lost forever," said one of the blue beings.

"Yes and we do need him for the future," said the other blue creature.

The blue creatures agreed with each other and started to help save Nick from the void.

Nick was almost fully in the void when he noticed the creatures making another circle appear around his face. Then he felt himself start to get pulled into another portal while his body was entering the void. Then he suddenly felt a little faint and blacked out. Nick's body had fully entered the void and as it drifted away from the vortex, it soon started to vanish. Although the blue creatures weren't sure if they had saved him or not, they decided to stay there for a while to try and work out a way to retrieve him if they had failed. They knew that he was important for the future so he needed to be saved. Nick didn't know where he was going as he fell through the time stream. He started to see random pictures appear in front of him as he fell into an image and flew in front a car with two women in it. He noticed confused expressions on their faces when his eye twitched, making him do a small wink as he vanished into another image. Then as he spun in circles, he noticed himself turn transparent and disappeared.

Nick started to wake up so he opened his eyes. He stood up, wondering where he was when he noticed Ben, Regen, and Bailey walking through the seaweed grass. He was half-angry at them for ditching him, but also glad that they were okay. Then as he ran to Regen to clip his ear, he missed. Then he ran in front of Bailey, but Bailey just walked past him. Confused, Nick ran in front of Ben and shouted at all of them, but Ben walked through him along with the others. Then as

Nick levitated, he realised the horrible truth. He was dead. In addition, was now a ghost.

The World Above
New Frontier
Chapter 7
The Hungry-Ones

Back in the World Below...
Michaela and Kate were on the road as they tried to set up the
radio, even when it had no connection to any services.
Eventually, they noticed that there weren't any internet
connections anywhere, so they just had to hope that everyone
they knew was okay.

They had been driving for about a day, making stops for food
and bathroom breaks along the way. Although they were glad
that they hadn't seen any more trenches, they also weren't
sure where a safe place was. And even though their breaks
may have taken longer than they should have, they were
switching drivers when they both noticed a strange blue light
appear in front of them.

The blur was blue and faint, causing Michaela to slow the car
down to a stop. Then suddenly a strange man appeared out of
the image and even though he didn't have legs, he still seemed
okay. In addition, as this strange man flew in front of them,
Kate noticed that he may have winked at them, while
Michaela noticed he didn't have fingers either. Then as
another blue blur appeared in front of him, he vanished into a
blue light and it all ended. Neither of them knew what that
was or why it was there, but they soon just decided that they
had imagined it... together at once.

Michaela immediately drove away from that area and decided to just forget about it when Kate spotted a town in front of them. As they drove through the town, they noticed that it was quiet and empty. All of the windows had been smashed on the houses and shops like the other towns, but this one seemed different from the others. Michaela drove the car slowly through the wreck of the town when Kate saw someone on the left running at them and screaming for help.

The woman opened up the backseat door and climbed inside before Michaela could lock all of the doors. Then the woman yelled at Michaela to turn the car around and drive away as someone else appeared out of the same house and ran to the car. This person had pointy looking teeth with long sharp fingernails as he jumped in front of the car, opened up the bonnet, and pulled apart a few wires in the motor, making it smoke up and break down. Then as this psycho person smiled at what he'd done, he walked over to the front door to meet Kate.

All of the doors were locked when the woman in the back tried to hide away. The person soon picked up a rock and threw it at the car window, placing many cracks in it. Michaela crawled to the back seat while Kate looked eye to eye at the person outside the car. Michaela searched the back to try and find some kind of weapon to keep this person away when she found something. The person then picked up the rock again and threw it through the window, just missing Kate as he reached in to unlock the car door.

The person climbed into the car, and as it gave a smile of victory, it leaped towards Kate when Michaela swung a hammer at his shoulder. The person fell to the side as they immediately climbed out of the car and ran away from him. The three of them ran through the town where they found a bakery with possibly some food in it.

"We need to be careful when we walk into this bakery," warned the woman. Confused, Michaela asked her what her name was and why it would be dangerous.
"My name is Tara and thank you for rescuing me by the way. The person that chased us had become a cannibal and was going to eat us. He was my brother...." After a small pause, she continued, "They're not like zombies where if they bite you, you become one of them, but they are still dangerous and everywhere as the need for food has affected almost everyone in this town and possibly most of the world. The impulse that turns you into a Hungry-One," said Tara.

As soon as Tara said this, they noticed someone running up to them for help when four hungry-ones were seen chasing after him. Michaela, Kate and Tara all ran into the bakery where they grabbed some food and saw a stairway to a second floor. As the three of them ran up the stairway, Tara heard some noises from the kitchen. Then someone got thrown across the counter with blood all over him and bite marks everywhere, followed by a hungry-one that appeared and gnawed through his neck.

The other guy running away from four hungry-ones opened up the shop door where he noticed the one at the counter. Before he knew it, the hungry-one leaped at him. He swiftly dodged it and ran past Kate, Michaela and Tara. The four of them ran up the stairway to the second floor, just as the four hungry-ones ran in and trampled all over the one on the ground. Then they ran upstairs to get the others.

Michaela still had the hammer as a weapon while Tara pulled a knife out of her pocket. Kate and the other guy ran up yelling that the others were coming as the four hungry-ones followed behind them. Then as one of the hungry-ones ran at Michaela, she hesitated at first, but soon came to terms with what was going to happen as she smashed the hammer at his arm, causing him to stumble over. Then Tara came along from behind and slit his throat.

"Tara, you killed him, h, he could've been saved," stammered Kate.
Michaela looked out the window and noticed that one more hungry-one was running into the bakery they were in. Tara then proceeded in dragging the dead hungry-one across the ground and tossed it down the stairs to knock over another one as Kate and Michaela starred in shock at the death they just witnessed.

Then Tara found a couch and got Michaela to go and help her push it down the stairs to stop the hungry-ones from attacking them. Kate and the guy that was with them looked around, trying to find something that could hold the hungry-ones off. As Michaela stood back from the stairway, she started to realise what sort of world she had now been introduced to and had an idea on how to stop the hungry-ones.

Michaela had passed the hammer to Kate since she didn't need it anymore. Then she asked Tara if she could use her knife. While Tara was reluctant at first, she gave it to her and followed Kate into a closet to hide. The other guy hid behind the bed. Then as Michaela stood in front of the window, three of the hungry-ones saw Michaela as they showed off menacing grins, and all ran at her.

As the hungry-ones were running, two of them jumped at her, just as Michaela jumped out of the way, making two of them fly out the window. The other one hit the edge of it, making it lay sprawled on the ground. Then as it looked at Michaela angrily, he reached to her and started to stand, when she used the knife to stab him in the arm. The guy looked out from behind the bed and stared at what Michaela had done. Then looked down at the hungry-one falling over with blood spilling onto the ground. Michaela was just realising what she had just done and realised she wasn't feeling guilty about it.

The guy decided to look out for more hungry-ones and went over to the stairway. Kate walked over to Michaela and said, "I can't believe you actually stabbed him."
"I couldn't either at first, but then I realised what sort of world we were living in and realised that I needed to adapt, in order to survive," said Michaela.
Then as Kate thought about the comment, the guy looked down the stairs as Tara yelled, "Vic, don't go down there."
"Don't worry 'T', I'll be fine."

Vic continued down the stairs and started to climb over the couch, when he suddenly felt something grab his leg, making him jump back in shock as one of the hungry-ones started to crawl from its hiding spot.

The hungry-one climbed over the couch as everyone was stepping backwards and preparing for the attack. Then as the hungry-one jumped at Tara, Vic ran in and spear tackled the hungry-one behind the couch.

All they heard was the screaming of the hungry-one as Vic shoved it down the stairs with him and behind a corner. Startled, the others ran over to help him and saw the shadows of what was happening to hungry-one on the back of the stairway. Then as it seemed Vic was holding the hungry-one back, spinning circles appeared around him.

Just as the hungry-one pushed him against the stairway, Tara ran down the stairs quickly before seeing Vic's shadow push kick the hungry-one down the stairs. Then Vic started to turn blue. When Tara saw Vic, she was confused of what was happening to him since his skin was a glowing blue colour. Then as he started to disappear, the hungry-one leapt towards him just as he vanished into a blue blur right in front of her, with the hungry-landing his face against the corner of one of the stairs.

Shocked from Vic's disappearance, Tara tried to scramble back up to the top of the stairs in panic, while the hungry-one down laid on the stairway without moving a muscle.
Near the top of the stairs, Kate and Michaela were preparing to walk down, when the hungry-one behind them that was stabbed in the arm stood up and ran at them.

As the hungry-one ran at them from behind, he was about to bite down on Michaela's neck, until she turned back and stabbed him in the chest. Then as Michaela pulled out the knife, the hungry-one collapsed to the floor as she stood still, realising that she had just killed someone. Kate immediately turned to her as they were both recovering from what had just happened.

"Michaela, are you okay?" asked Kate.
"I think I'm fine. I did it to ensure my survival. We're living in a new world now Kate, and I think I just realised that survival is key, whether or not the decisions made are adequate or not."
"But, you killed someo…"
"Survival is key."
Then as Michaela cut Kate off with her sentence, she followed Tara down the stairs.

After seeing Vic seemingly vanish, Tara started to crawl down the stairs to work out where he was and couldn't find him anywhere. Then as spinning circles caused her to believe he had been killed by the hungry-one, she tried not to think about what had happened since death was becoming a normal thing, and eventually they would have to get used to it, whether they wanted to or not. Then as they looked around the corner of the stairs, they saw the knocked out hungry-one and the trampled on hungry-one with a face covered in blood and eating someone's arm.

Immediately, Tara grabbed back her knife from Michaela, ran down, properly killed the one on the stairs and threw the knife at the hungry-one's head, leaving it sprawled on the ground. Kate couldn't even look at the dead bodies on the ground as Michaela was adjusting her way of thinking to her surroundings. They were all weary walking down to the first floor and into suburbia, so Michaela thought that there could have been a back door for them to escape through.

Michaela found the back door, opened it and saw an alleyway they could run into. Then as she looked around, she started to hear some groaning up and down the alley and that's when she saw some dark figures appear and walk towards her. Then she saw the two other hungry-ones that fell out the window as they also started to crawl to her with their broken legs. Michaela realised they needed another way of escaping and as she shut the door, she stepped backwards and listened as the hungry-ones attempted to shove things towards the door.

Kate and Tara were walking to the back until Michaela told them that it was more dangerous out there than it would be in suburbia. Immediately, Kate, Michaela and Tara ran out of the shop, just as the hungry-ones at the back door eventually broke it down and immediately crowded through it, following the scent of their next feast.

Kate, Michaela and Tara were running away from the shop when they noticed a bunch of skeletons covered in blood and guts on the sidewalks and in the houses. They all started to hear more groaning around them as more hungry-ones were emerging everywhere. Then when they looked behind, they noticed at least twenty hungry-ones chasing after them. Kate, Michaela and Tara were running as hard as they could, just as a car appeared nearby with spinning circles surrounding it. Even though they weren't sure if it would run or not, they figured they had no other choice and tried to start it anyway.

The keys were in the car ready to be used and they all shut their doors to start it up. The hungry-ones were getting closer to them when the car started up and drove off. As they were driving, they were beginning to notice more hungry-ones joining the group behind them as they exited their houses.

Then as more of them came, the closer they got to the car. The hungry-ones had gotten faster than any ordinary person. Then when they were close enough, they started to jump onto the car.

The hungry-one punched a hole inside the boot of the car to prove how strong he was. Then a female hungry-one jumped at the door and punched her hand through the window with a rock in her hand. The hungry-ones were running faster when Michaela sped up the car. Then two more hungry-ones jumped onto the boot and climbed on top of it. The hungry-ones on top of the car started to cut holes through the roof with knives and opened it up.

The hungry-ones were about to jump in when Michaela swerved the car around throwing the two of them off, but allowing a few more to latch on. Tara looked at the back and noticed two guns with spinning circles around them. She immediately grabbed them and threw one to Kate. Then as Tara started to fire the gun, Kate looked over at her killing everyone surrounding her and realised that they had the same goal as the hungry-ones. They all just wanted to survive, even if it meant everyone else had to die.

Then as she looked down and noticed a gun in her lap, she picked it up, uncertain of what she should do next. Michaela was zig-zagging to shake the hungry-ones off as Tara looked at Kate, wondering why she wasn't helping with shooting down the hungry-ones. Then as more hungry-ones appeared around the car, they started to jump for the wheels.

Some spinning circles appeared around all of them as some of the hungry-ones stayed back to eat the dead ones sprawled all over the road. Then as more spinning circles appeared around them, the hungry-ones leaped for the wheels and popped them. The hungry-ones on the roof fell into the bonnet making fuel begin to leak out. Then the car slowed to a stop and the hungry-ones pulled open the car doors and jumped at them.

Michaela was thrown a gun from Kate as she still didn't feel comfortable killing anyone. Then as Michaela was shooting the ones on her side, Tara shot at the ones on the roof as Kate looked around and heard all the screams and thumps as the hungry-ones fell off the car and onto the road in agony. The hungry-ones were punching their way through the back and front when a hungry-one dodged the bullets and leaped onto Michaela. The hungry-one was frantically trying to bite her as she held him away from her face, causing Kate to realise she needed to help out somehow.

The hungry-one was digging its nails into Michaela's skin as she dropped the gun and held it back. Tara was next to her, firing at the hungry-ones running everywhere. Then as Michaela's hand slipped, Kate reached forward and shoved it off her. It hit the side of the car as Michaela picked up the gun, and fired a bullet through its head.
Kate still couldn't believe what Michaela was doing as she'd never seen her this violent before.

Then as blood was soaking into Michaela's clothes, a blue light appeared around them. Then as the hungry-ones had surrounded the car, the guns only had a few bullets left, just as the group vanished, leaving a spark to slowly flow down to the ground that was covered in spilled petrol.

The World Above
New Frontier
Chapter 8
The Guy in the Shadows

The group re-appeared again wondering how they teleported or who teleported them when they noticed a massive explosion in the distance as they saw people's dead bodies land on the ground, burnt to a crisp. They watched as the car got blasted apart as bits of the hungry-ones and car parts were falling to the ground around the town.

Then Kate noticed that bits of the hungry-ones and the car were also flying at them as she turned away from the disturbing sight. The three of them ran away from the falling debris as other people just hid in their houses. The debris from the explosion landed around the area, but didn't harm them as they dodged it all and ran off to try and escape that town. After running for a while, struggling to find any ways of transport, Michaela spotted a car in someone's garage. They didn't really want to risk finding more hungry-ones around there, but they also didn't want to have to walk either.

The three of them ran to the car when they noticed that the keys weren't in the ignition. They almost didn't want to risk walking into the house until Tara stated that it was getting late and that it would get dark soon. Although Kate and Michaela didn't really know if they could trust Tara, they decided to help find the keys. They looked around the house to find them, but they were nowhere to be seen. It was almost an impossibility for them to find the keys as the owner probably still had them for some reason. Then that was when Kate heard some shuffling in the distance with sparks going off.

There was still a room that they hadn't checked yet, but it was filled with darkness and spinning circles in the distance as a mysterious person emerged from the shadows with a set of keys in his hand. The guy appeared confused as he stumbled all over the place as if he was lost.

He didn't seem like a hungry-one, but when he saw Kate and Michaela, he gave a sigh of relief.

"I can't believe it worked again, and I found you all. Look, I know that you don't know who I am, but you have to trust that I know what I'm saying and that you need to c…" The guy immediately stopped what he was saying because the others were starting to step back in confusion. Then he had an idea by saying, "Look, I have the keys to the car and I know where there is a safe place we can go to. Kate wasn't very sure about this when Tara walked over to him, asked where they were going and if he had a map.

Tara looked at where they were going and figured that it may be a safe place to go to. And none of them really wanted to be walking around in the darkness. So they accepted the guys offer as they all headed into the car to drive along the road. The guy was happy with these arrangements as long as he drove, and everyone was okay with that, kind of, and Kate and Michaela could trust him about as much as they trusted Tara so they were fine with it.
"Hey Tara, do you know what those hungry-ones are?" asked Kate.

"Kind of, so far a fair amount of people had been getting really hungry, and even though it doesn't affect everyone, it does take over people's minds. Kind of like how hungry fish would eat other fish when they were hungry. The hunger changes the person into an uncontrollable monster that would be willing to eat anyone. It already affected my brother, and he tried to kill me... I don't know if this hunger disease can be cured, but from what I've experienced, it can affect anyone. We're always in danger, even when we think we're not."

"So you and Michaela were potentially killing people that could've been saved?" asked Kate.
"No. They were going to eat us and we had to defend ourselves. You should have been helping us out as well," said Michaela.
"I know, but..."
"But nothing, you nearly let me die at the hands of the hungry-one at some point!" Yelled Michaela.
"I just wasn't sure what to do."
"Next time, just kill it. This is a different world now, and we have to work together in order to survive. Are you able to help us survive?"
"Yeah, yes, definitely."
Then when you need to, just kill it. Our group's survival takes top priority."
"Okay, I understand now."

Tara and the guy felt like it was best to stay out of that conversation as the guy seemed pretty nervous about what was going on. Everyone decided to eat some of the food they took from the Bakery since they didn't want to risk being too hungry. Then as he drove down the road following the map the best he could since no one really knew what to talk about after that. There didn't seem to be any danger around so he decided to start up a conversation by asking, "By the way, my names Ben. Where are you guys from?

The World Above
New Frontier
Chapter 9
The Combined Beings

In the World Above…

The fish leaned over to stand up when he suddenly felt limp on his left side of the body. He looked at himself and didn't feel any different. He started to walk into the house, without realising that the other originally headless humans on the chopping board had vanished into a blue blur as well. Then he looked over his arms, noticing that they were changing colour with his legs. As he stumbled around, he realised he was having trouble seeing out of his left eye. He stumbled into the house and ran to the phone. Then as he ran past the mirror, he yelled out for his wife to come out.

He grabbed the phone and called for an ambulance to come and help him. He fell over in pain when he heard another voice next to him start to talk with half of his mouth. The fish still noticed that human skin was still getting absorbed into him when his wife ran out and fainted at the sight of him. He wasn't sure what to do as he bent down to help his wife. Then he lay next to her to rest, hoping that this would soon end.

Nick floated around the others who were walking through the grass as he realised no matter how much he tried, he couldn't get their attention. Then he turned around and noticed that more amphipods were chasing after them. Nick tried to warn the others, but he couldn't touch them. Then as he was trying to warn them, he stopped levitating and fell into the ground.

He noticed that his feet were stuck in the ground and he was still falling.

He tried to float back up, but couldn't. And as he fell further into the ground, the amphipods ran through his head and arms. Then in a desperate attempt, he tried to grab one of the amphipods and his hand disappeared into it. Then his arm got pulled into it. Then all of him got pulled out of the ground and disappeared into it. When Nick was gone, the amphipod turned limp and collapsed to the floor.

Nick opened his eyes and noticed that he was in a pale white room now. When he looked down, he noticed an amphipod in front of him, but smaller. Then he started to get stronger. As the little critter was trying to bite Nick, he picked it up and crushed it. Then he started to grow bigger and blacked out. He opened his eyes again, but couldn't move his fingers. He walked around and felt really different from usual. Nick had turned into an amphipod.

Nick looked at what he had become and decided to find the others. He ran over the amphipods heads as he searched the area. He was a little faster than the others and was walking over the critters in a big rush. Eventually, he was getting closer to the front of the pack and he saw the others feet. Then he remembered the way that they just ditched him when he was in trouble. And how much anger he now had for them.

Bailey and Ben were at the front pushing their way through the seaweed while Regen was running backwards kicking away the amphipods. Nick saw them and ran to the left to cut around while the other amphipods got kicked away. Ben, Bailey and Regen eventually found an opening in the seaweed and they ran across a concrete path. They thought that they had escaped the amphipods. Then they noticed some kind of tar on the road, but it looked more like snail slime.

Nick noticed the others in the opening and saw how all the other amphipods weren't going onto the concrete-like ground. He wasn't really sure why, but when he saw the tar-like stuff on the road, he realised the critters didn't want to risk getting stuck in it. Then he heard a siren in the distance sounding like a police or ambulance siren. Bailey was stepping back, acting cautiously when he accidentally stepped in the tar-like substance.

Regen looked back at the house, noticing that the front door was beginning to open. He started to turn back to the others to warn them when he saw Ben trying to get Bailey's foot out of the tar. Nick was watching them struggle when he noticed a brighter shade of light and the sirens sounding closer than before.
The fish started to open his one eye as the other one couldn't be opened. He got himself up and walked to the front door, knowing that the ambulance would be there quite soon. He started to open the door when he realised his other eye was beginning to open. He had control of his body, but he didn't have full control before he fainted. Frazer was beginning to wake up, wondering where he was and how he survived, even when he didn't feel like he could control his whole body.

Part of Nick hated them for letting him die, but the other half of him wanted them to live. He immediately ran across the road hoping to scare them back into the seaweed or whatever was behind the fence. He sensed that something was heading towards them and that they were all in danger.

Bailey managed to get his foot out of the tar-like stuff with Regen and Ben pulling him along. The fish managed to turn the handle and open the door. He went staggering out of the house and noticed the ambulance driving up the street. Then he looked down and saw the humans that got away, but instead of chasing after them, he stood away from them and hoped that they didn't go near him.

Regen noticed an amphipod walking towards them not knowing why the others weren't following behind it. Nick was trying to act scarier than the others by making faces and running around crazily. Ben, Bailey and Regen were running up the concrete to get around the fence. Nick followed behind them and was trying to get around the fence too.

They were getting closer to what looked like a footpath when a giant sea carcumber was pulling into the driveway with blue and red sirens above it. Then the fish that looked kind of human was running towards the sea carcumber stumbling and limping. Ben and Regen made it to the path while Bailey followed behind.

Nick was smaller and slower than the others were. Then as the sea carcumber drove past the footpath, he noticed some sort of wheel on the side of the sea carcumber and realised that he wouldn't be able to make it as an amphipod. The wheel was about to crush him. He leaped out of the amphipods body and levitated in the seaweed. It immediately fell lifeless to the ground making Nick wonder if it would even wake up. Then the wheel of the sea carcumber crushed it.

Nick levitated above the seaweed and floated in the air. He noticed the sea carcumber stop in the driveway, allowing two more fish to jump out and help the other one stumbling around. Nick decided to ignore them and float over to the others to see if they were okay, when he started to lose feeling in his fingers.

Frazer, and the fish he was part of were stumbling over to the two ambulance fish when Frazer pulled back because he didn't want fish examining him. The two fish grabbed Frazer because his fish half was allowing them to examine him. Nick turned around, being somewhat curious about what was happening when the two fish had the injured one on a stretcher and were placing it in the back of their ambulance carcumber. The last thing Nick saw of them was some glowing green circle around the fish-human person.

Ben and the others walked along the path when he noticed part of the fence blow up in the distance. They ran to the scattered planks of the fence when Nick flew over to them and was about to possess Bailey, until he started to think about something. He looked at his arm and noticed that his hand was gone. He needed a body to keep his spirit whole or else he'd die. He wanted to possess Bailey, Regen or Ben just so he could live, until he remembered how lifeless the amphipod was when he left it.

Jared and Harry jumped off Toms' arm as Jared fell over, and Harry tried to keep his balance. Tom stared down the wooden fence and made his arm grow stronger, and punched his hand through the fence. The wooden fence wasn't actually that hard to punch through. Harry tried to walk forward until he realised he was standing in a puddle of air.

Then when Tom stayed standing and Jared stood up fine as well, Harry realised he still couldn't leave the group yet and walked onto the robot arm. They walked onto the path where they saw Ben, Bailey and Regen. When they wondered where Nick was, they just had to assume the worst.

Nick was watching Tom and the others walk through what looked like an explosion from a distance, when he noticed that his feet had disappeared as well. He had to find a body to possess. Bailey, Ben and Regen ran up to Tom, Jared and Harry, and after a bit of a rush, he decided to possess Regen.

He started to float towards Regen, glided past everyone and was just about to possess him... until a strong wind came and blew him away from Regen and into Tom's body.

The World Above
New Frontier
Chapter 10
Within the Mind

Tom felt a cold breeze flow through him. His eyes shut and he just stopped moving. The robot arm continued to walk everyone around while Tom was pretty much knocked out. When Tom opened his eyes, he was in a blank, pale room and started to look around. Then as he looked closer inside the room, he noticed a face appearing with massive arms and ghostly legs. Then as the monster looked down on Tom, it leaned towards him for the kill.

Tom immediately pushed his robot hand into the ground and propelled himself into the air. The ghostly monster tried to grab Tom so he punched the ghostly monster in the nose, causing it to step backwards in pain. Then after recovery, leaned forward to soon grab him again. As the monster's hand was reaching for Tom, Tom grabbed its arm, smashed it against the ground, and ran up it. Tom turned his robot arm into a long blade and stuck it into the monster's arm as he ran up it. Then when he got to its shoulder, he stabbed it in the head.

Nick stepped back in pain as Tom jumped back to the ground again. Nick was about to give up possessing Tom when he turned his robot arm into a rocket launcher. Then as Nick started to escape Toms mind, he stepped through the wall and saw darkness. Tom opened his eyes as he was now conscious again, wondering what had happened to him, but decided to ignore it and just think he imagined it.

Nick reappeared again, but had lost his arms and part of his legs. Even though he was confused on how he lost to Tom, the next person he saw was Adam so he flew into him.
Adam found a hole in the fence. He looked around and noticed more beach worms heading towards them. Adam had Rusheel, Josh and Seth standing in his giant hands as he ran for the fence. The beach worms were still scratching Adams legs with their teeth with no scratch marks appearing.

Adam ran through the fence while the others ducked under it. They noticed the others running towards them as Toms group was closer.

While Rusheel turned back to make sure the dirt worms weren't chasing them, he turned back to see Tom seem to wake up from a sleep. Tom looked up at them wondering what was happening to Adam. Nick was staring in the same position as Tom and started to try and understand Adam's situation.

Adam felt a cold breeze flow through him, but that's all he felt. He felt colder than usual and a little sleepy, but he was still conscious and just figured he was tired.

Nick opened his eyes and noticed that he was in a darker shaded room. Although he was wondering why Adams mind was different to the others, he noticed two glowing red eyes and a big smirking mouth. Then he noticed the room get darker as clawed arms appeared on the walls spreading towards him. Then as Nick stared into the face of the darkness, he noticed a small body in it.

"What are you doing trying to possess someone that's already possessed by me? No one disturbs a spirit's work so you will die for good this time," yelled the darkness. Then as the darkness spread towards Nick, he knew that trying to possess Adam would be a bad idea as that little body inside the darkness was Adams spirit. Nick started to push himself through the wall of Adams mind and fell through just before the darkness reached him.

Nick had completely lost his arms and legs while his body and part of his head was disappearing. He looked around and saw Josh as his last chance to live. Adam was able to stay wide-awake again, even though he was a little dazed and confused. Nick flew into Josh, making him collapse in Adams giant hand. Nick noticed that he was in a pale room again and saw Josh's body in front of him. Nick knew that by doing this, Josh would most likely be killed, but without thinking, he started to reach for Josh and crush his body so he could live.

Josh woke up dazed and saw a massive monster in front of him. Then as it tried to reach for him, he jumped out of the way, but the monsters other hand reached out and grabbed him. Josh was desperately struggling to escape as he felt his body vanishing around him. Then as the monster started to shape into Josh, the last words Josh heard from Nick was "I'm sorry… I will rescue you soon," then it all ended. Josh was crushed in Nick's hand and Nick woke up in Josh's body, amazed that he was alive.

He woke up and noticed that everyone was staring at him. Nick stood up looking at his hands and legs and realised that he was truly in Josh's body. Seth stood near him and asked if he was okay, and without thinking, Nick answered with "I'm fine, I just fainted from all the stuff that has happened to us." No one knew what to think about his answer, so they just figured that that was what he did. Everyone continued to walk down the street and while Nick was happy to be alive, he knew that he still had to find Josh though. He had to be somewhere.

Josh opened his eyes wondering where he was, but even when he saw the place, he still wasn't sure. He seemed to be in some kind of sphere that he couldn't get out of. If he stuck his hand through one side of the sphere, his hand would appear on the other side. If he reached the top of the sphere, his hand would appear in the ground. All around him, he noticed strange lines of light passing around him. The lines were everywhere around him, but except for that, all he saw was darkness... endless darkness.

Nick stood in Adams' hand with Seth next to him and Rusheel on the other hand as Adam carried them all across the street. Next to them was Tom letting his robot arm crawl across the ground allowing Jared and Harry to follow the others. Ben, Bailey and Regen were still feeling guilty about how they left Nick behind. Frazer was carried into the back of the sea carcumber with the fish still part of him when Lily and his wife ran out of the house to check on him.

Lily was starting to tear up when she saw what had happened to her dad. Her mum was trying to comfort her and make sure she was okay. As everyone was walking away, Ben turned around and noticed the state that the fish were in and kind of hoped that they would get better again. After all, they seemed to be trying to survive. He just hoped that they would stop humaning and eat something other than people. Then as Lily looked up at her father, she noticed some green circles spinning around him.

Frazer was finding it harder to struggle as the spinning green circles spun faster around him. His wife and daughter had worried looks on their faces as Frazer started to separate from the fish. Even though they were separating, their bodies were just being reversed in time, making Frazer reappear dead and headless on the ground.

The fish had become completely fine again. Then he looked across and saw the humans walking down the path, wondering how they were able to walk. Eventually, the fish got out of the sea carcumber and followed his wife and daughter into the house, not wanting to go humaning again. And as the ambulance seacarcumber drove off, the little amphipods crawled towards Frazer's dead body for a snack. Just before the amphipods crawled over him, a green circle emerged around his body; re winded him in time so that he could breathe again, and caused him to vanish into a blue light.

Nick noticed that everyone was just walking along when he found this as his opportunity to search for Josh. Nick shut his eyes and as he rolled his eyes back, he ended up looking into his mind where the next thing he saw was a brain. He didn't know that he could do this as a ghost but he was still getting used to his new powers. He tried to look over Josh's brain, trying to find some kind of memory that was about Josh, but all he could see was his own memories. He was afraid that Josh was gone for good and that he couldn't be saved.

As Adam was walking, he noticed some kind of image was forming inside his head again. Then as the image formed in his head, he noticed a huge smirking face in front of him with glowing red eyes. The face seemed to be made up of swirls of dark shaded colours, but this being looked like it could be dangerous. Then as Adam looked closer at the image, he noticed something inside the mouth of the face. He looked closer and saw a body inside it. Then as the image faded away, Adam could see properly again and heard another message in his head with the repeating words, "Your looped, your looped, YOUR LOOPED!

Nick searched more inside Josh's brain to find anything that represented Josh in any way. He briefly searched through all of the lobes of his brain when he decided to start exploring the centre of it. Nick tried to search the centre of the brain and all he was seeing was flesh and chemical messages shooting past him in lines of light. Then as he got closer to the very centre of the brain, he noticed a tiny circle in the middle of the chemical messages shooting past him.

Josh stood where he was in the circle surrounded by endless darkness, trying to figure out what had happened to him. Then he noticed something in the distance that wasn't like the darkness he was surrounded in. The thing in the distance slowly grew a face as it drifted closer to him. Then Josh noticed massive claws surrounding him and heard it begin to speak to him.

As Nick got closer to the tiny circle he was beginning to realise he had become microscopic. The chemical messages were getting increasing in size around him, as blood cells were appearing massive. Nick was finally able to get a better look at the tiny circle and saw Josh standing there.

"Josh I'm here to save you. It's just me Nick, and I needed to borrow your body so I could live."

Josh wasn't sure what to think about this or how it was even possible, but then he noticed Nick grab the sphere and start to pull it away. As the sphere was being pulled away, Josh noticed that the circle was beginning to get smaller, and the smaller the circle got, the more crushed Josh would be. Josh's arms had gone through the wall and his hands went through the wall again while his head was in the roof making his head appear on the ground. Nick noticed Josh was tangled and immediately let go of the circle, allowing Josh to be whole again as it floated back to where it was.

Nick wasn't going to give up on trying to rescue Josh, but he had to leave to make sure no one was suspicious of him. Nick only had one more idea on how to release Josh and that was to rip open the circle. Nick grabbed the sides of the sphere with his hands, and as his fingers dug into the circle, he tried to pull it open. Josh noticed the sphere begin to rip open, but it was also shrinking as well. Josh yelled at Nick to hurry up as his legs were through the roof and ground while his arms had gone through the same side at least three times.

Nick had created a gap in the tinier circle and Josh's head and body were getting crushed against his arms and legs, but before he was about to splatter, he slid through the gap in the circle and fell into the eternal mind. Nick tried to grab him but

Josh just fell through his hand. Josh soon vanished and without any other option, Nick had to return to the world again. He got himself out of the centre of the brain as the chemical messages soon vanished and he looked at a full brain again. Then as he looked back into his eyes, he turned them the right way round again and saw everyone looking at him.

Rusheel and Seth were looking at Josh wondering if he was okay. The others ran over to see what was going on when they noticed Josh opening his eyes again, wondering why everyone was looking at him.
"Are you okay Josh?" Asked Rusheel.
"Yes... I am fine because I am Josh," stuttered Josh.
"What happened to you? That's the second time today you've collapsed," said Seth.
"I... I...was just resting a little, that's all... I mean I'm absolutely fine because I'm all normal and Josh," stuttered Josh.

No one was sure what to think about this and they didn't really know him that much so they figured that that was how he acted regularly, and just let him act the way he did. Nick knew that he may have stuffed up acting like Josh, but he didn't even know if he could get him back, so he was beginning to think that maybe he'd have to stay in Josh's body forever. As he stood in Adam's giant hand, he noticed that they had reached the corner of the street and seeing a bunch of shops in front of them, realised that they would need to split up to collect things to survive.

Josh was falling in complete darkness, even when he didn't feel like he was even falling anymore. He felt like he was just levitating mid-air. Then he noticed the chemical messages begin to get smaller and distant as he realised he was slowly growing bigger. Then as he grew, he noticed he was appearing in the middle of something fleshy.

As he levitated out of the fleshy thing, he was growing to the size of his brain. Everything got paler and he realised he was back in the mind again. With nowhere to go and nothing to do to get out.

While all of them were working out their groups and where they would go, Nick was still getting used to his new body and Josh was trying to think of a way to escape. Then a thought came to Nick. What happened to his body? Where did it go?
Nick's body was still floating around in the void, lifeless and limp as it was slowly becoming forgotten, and was fading away from existence.

The World Above
New Frontier
Chapter 11
Human Trawling Boat

Meanwhile, in the World Below…

"Have you experienced the hungry-ones yet Ben?" asked Tara.

"Yeah, some of my mates became cannibals, or hungry-ones as you call them. I'm amazed I'm still alive after going through the things I've done so far."

"Same with all of us I think," said Tara.

Then Ben stated where he was going so everyone agreed with him. They were heading to an airport so that they could escape to New South Wales Australia, where they would go to the safe place and never be in danger again.

As they were driving along, watching out for more of the hungry-ones, Michaela noticed some object in the sky. Kate and Tara had already noticed this and asked Ben if he knew what it was. Ben just said that it was a humaning boat and that they should just stay away from it. Then they noticed some people running towards them, followed by a whole stampede of people. Ben immediately tried to turn the car around, but as they started to drive away, a crowd of people was running at the car.

Not knowing whether these people had become a hungry-one or not, Ben locked all of the doors, right after three people had already gotten into the car and were yelling at Ben to start driving. They didn't look like hungry-ones, but when Ben looked in front, he guessed that something much worse than hungry-ones or trenches was heading towards them. It was a giant net being dragged behind some kind human trawling boat.

The net swept across the land, picking up anyone that got in its way. Then before Ben could turn the car around, he started to drive backwards, causing the crowd to give up on the car and run off. Kate pointed out whether he needed to go left or right, as she didn't want him to hit anyone. Then the three people who'd just jumped in, frantically climbed over the chairs into the boot of the car. The stampede of people was catching up to them and were running around the car. A bunch of people started to climb over the car, but Ben continued to drive backwards and increase the speed.

Tara noticed that the boat-shaped thing in the sky was above them now with the net trailing behind it. As people ran around the car, Kate and Michaela went to try and search the back of the car for some kind of weapons. The people running along in front of them were desperate to escape, and when someone tried to climb up the boot, he slipped and got run over. Tara looked forward and noticed that the net was like a spider web. If you got caught in it, you couldn't escape. And it had nearly reached them!

Tara quickly yelled at Ben to turn left so that they could drive to the side and not away from it. Ben turned the wheel and as they turned left, Michaela saw a dead blood coated body come flying towards them and land on the ground as one of the hungry-ones appeared in the crowd and jumped at someone else. Then Michaela looked over at Kate, handed her the gun, and said, "Use this if necessary, my life is in your hands."

Kate then started to breathe in and out repeatedly as she held the gun. She saw dead bodies sprawled around the place with other people running over them.

The boot was opened by someone and Ben yelled out "Hey, Darian, I knew I'd be able to recognise you. Go get your friends and make sure no one else gets in since most of the people here are really hungry."
Although no one knew how he knew her name, they weren't really concerned about it, but instead were making sure that they didn't get thrown out of the car. Then Darian looked over at her friends, Kelly and Amilia, and wondered why Ben didn't recognise them as well.

Michaela and Kate noticed that they had almost escaped the net until another hungry-one came and threw a sharp rock at the windscreen and cracked it a little. The car ran over another dead body and bounced Kelly into Amilia, causing them both to start rolling out of the car. Darian immediately went to reach for Kelly and Amilia as she started to slide out of the car with them.

Then before any of them realised it, a knife started to cut through the car roof and rip it open.
Ben pushed down on the gas pedal as hard as he could as a hungry-one was looking down on Kate through the roof. Then as Tara pulled out her gun, she fired a bullet through the hungry-one that tried to leap towards the bonnet. Then as the hungry-one on the roof was able to fit through the hole, Kate had her finger on the trigger and planned to purposely miss to hopefully scare the hungry-one off. That was when Ben drove over a big rock, jolting Kate into the air and firing it through the hungry-one's eye, making it fall off the car.

The net caught the front of the car, making it get slung sideways across the net, causing Amilia's foot to get caught in it also. The car stopped running and they were hoisted into the air with the other hundred people caught in it also. Then Ben looked behind and yelled, "Darian, it's a shield, you'll need it soon."

Then as the car tilted, Darian grabbed the shield from the back of the car just as Tara fell out and slid down the edge of the net. As Ben followed, he immediately twisted and pulled out the car keys before he fell out of the car. He quickly put them in his pocket and followed Tara down the net.

Michaela looked at Kate, realising Kate had just killed someone as she checked behind them and saw that Darian, Kelly and Amilia were pulled out of the car and got attached to the net. Then Michaela climbed into the front seat, but realised that the car had been completely shifted onto the net and that they couldn't run away anymore.

Kate sat still, trying to contemplate what she had accidentally done as the net was being lifted into the air. Then as Michaela realised they had to jump, Kate looked at her as she stood next to her best friend. Then as they jumped out, they grabbed onto the edge of the net that wasn't as sticky as the middle and slid to the bottom.

Ben and Tara ran over to Kate and Michaela to make sure they were okay. Even though they were all limping a little, they realised that that was the least of their problems as they saw how many people were caught in the net and were getting hoisted into the sky. Ben knew they were going to get separated from Darian somehow. All he could hope was that they would somehow meet the other version of his self, and continue the loop.

He did think about something else though. For a while, Ben was starting to accept the fish as beings trying to survive the best they could. He saw them as villains, but villains with the same intentions as humans did in the past. But what he just witnessed was unforgivable. He just watched fish capture hundreds to thousands of people seemingly without a thought. After seeing this, his hatred of the fish increased. He could never forgive them for their actions. No one who saw this could forgive their actions. The fish were defiantly the enemy, and nothing could ever change that.

None of them really cared about how Ben knew the other person's name as Michaela walked over to Kate and said, "Killing someone shocked me as well at first, but you'll get used to it. Just remember this. Survival is key, whether or not the decisions made are adequate or not. And you'll be fine." Kate would have been fine from that, but she shot the bullet by mistake, and she now knew that she could never get used to it. It just didn't seem right.

They didn't have a car anymore, but they still had their lives. Then as they started to walk, a bunch of spinning circles appeared around them when Ben said, "Everyone, stand completely still."
Although they weren't very sure on why they needed to stand still, they just did because Ben said they should. Then as more spinning circles appeared around them, a blurred light appeared, causing them to start feeling dizzy. They all soon fainted and vanished into a blue light.

Michaela started to wake up first. Then everyone else woke up, wondering where they were. Ben immediately stood up and told everyone to start running to the plane. No one really understood how he knew where he was or why he wanted to go on the plane. But they didn't know where they were, and because they didn't want to get lost, they followed behind him.

It was great that everyone was following Ben the whole time. It meant that everything could go to plan.

Back in the human trawling net...
Darian, Kelly and Amilia grabbed each other's hands to make sure they couldn't lose each other as a group of other people was pushed into them. They were hoisted into the World Above which was made up of water and traces of oxygen. Then suddenly everyone was struggling to breathe. Darian looked through a gap in the net and noticed a boat like thing that was blurred since she was under water. Darian recognised this as the way we hunted fish and kind of remembered it being called 'Boat Trawling'.

The net got hauled over onto the boat and a trap door on the deck opened. Everyone got dropped into it and landed with a loud thud. Kelly and Amilia were being crushed under the pile of people, but the air in this area was breathable so they were kind of okay. Darian was trying to break free through the net, but soon gave up as a bunch of people fell on her. Then the trap door shut on them and all of the oxygen was being used quickly from everyone yelling for help and panicking

As the oxygen was being used up, Kelly slowly let go of Amilia and Darian as they started to feel a little faint and separated. Then as they realised they were separating, they frantically tried to reach for one another. As people got in the way, other people were also getting pushed out of the way. Then as they were just about to grab each other's hands, they started to pass out from the limited amount of oxygen in the boats hull.

Darian kept her eyes open to see where she was and saw the net get lifted into the air to soon be dropped again to gain another catch of humans. Then as she looked forward, she saw an opening and watched as everyone was getting pulled through it. She felt weak all over, noticed Kelly up front and tried to yell out to her, but didn't have the strength to do so. Then she also noticed Amilia nearby as well. Darian wasn't sure where the opening led as she noticed some cars around the hatch, with fish standing upright and pulling the cars out with their hands.

Then Darian remembered the gadget that the guy gave her. He said it was some kind of shield so she looked it over and noticed a button. Then she fell down a step and landed closer to Kelly. Darian nearly dropped the gadget, but hung on to it and pushed a button that activated it. It glowed and Darian could breathe properly again. There was some kind of shield around her now. She looked forward and noticed that people were falling off the edge of a bench.

She immediately looked around for Kelly and Amilia when she realised Amilia was close by, reached out for her hand and grabbed it, allowing the shield to spread across the two of them. Then when she noticed Kelly getting swept closer to the edge. Darian and Amilia tried to crawl closer to her as helpless people surrounded her struggling to breathe.

As people fell off the edge, they didn't seem to be fighting back. Then when Darian and Amilia crawled over to her, they reactivated the shield around her, allowing her to give a sigh of relief. Then before the three of them knew it, they fell off the edge and landed on a conveyor belt leading somewhere else.

The World Above
New Frontier
Chapter 12
Splitting Up

Back in the World Above…
Ben, Bailey and Regen decided to go as a group while Tom, Jared and Harry were going to go as another group. Adam, Seth, Josh and Rusheel made the third group. Ben, Bailey and Regen were going to the supermarket to get food while Adam, Seth, Josh and Rusheel were heading off to an airquarium to find some more air to breathe in. Tom, Jared and Harry were going to a humaning store to find some weapons to fight off the fish.

Ben's group ran across the road to the supermarket with Adams group following behind them. Tom's group however, had a little more trouble crossing the road than the others as his robot arm was slower than the others and many cars were driving past.

Ben, Bailey and Regen jumped over sea carcumber tar as they ran across the road. Adam picked up a little more speed than the others and carried Seth, Josh and Rusheel over the road to the airquarium. Tom's group had to work out another way to cross the road and had an idea. He got Jared and Harry off his robot arm and they both immediately slipped up.

Then as Harry continued to try and stand up straight and walk by himself, Tom hoisted himself into the air and got Jared to stand on the robot arm, while hanging on to it. Then Tom started to run across the road with his robot arm. Sea carcumbers were driving around everywhere with sticky tar all over the road. Jared hung on tight even though he was starting to slip. Tom landed again and saw a sea carcumber drive over him. Tom got knocked over and Jared was desperately trying to hang on. All they saw was darkness. They didn't know how they could continue onwards.

Ben, Bailey and Regen were running through some seaweed when they noticed some kind of footpath heading into a Corals store. They turned around and noticed Adam's group going into the airquarium. Then Ben signalled his group to stay close so that the shield didn't break. As they ran across the path, they saw what looked like a bin and decided to hide under it. As they ran to it, they noticed some fish walk out in front of them. They all stood back and let the fish walk past. Then when they thought it was safe, they started to run to the bin.

Adam was carrying Rusheel, Seth and Josh with his unusually massive hands and they were heading over to the airquarium. They figured it was an airquarium because they saw a tank with some humans in it. As Nick was standing there, he looked through the glass door and noticed some sort of counter as well. But the shop seemed too small to be an airquarium. Josh was just sitting in Nicks mind while Nick was controlling his body. As Josh paced the mind within Nicks' head, he came up with an idea on how he could escape, but he'd need Nick's help to succeed.

Nick stood back as Adam was slowly opening the door to the airquarium. Then Nick heard a voice in his head.

"Dude I'm still alive so don't just shut me out of your head." Nick wasn't sure if he was hearing voices or not until he started to recognise the voice. Josh was still speaking to him! Nick wanted to make sure he wasn't just imagining it so he rolled his eyes back and looked into his head. He searched through his brain when Josh yelled that he was inside Nicks mind again.

Nick didn't really know how he could enter the mind again so he decided to get out of his head. "I don't know how to visit you Josh, but I can still hear you. As Nick listened to Josh, it turned out he had a plan to escape and he was agreeing with everything Josh was saying, while thinking of something else at the same time. If Josh did manage to escape, who would inhabit the body?

The sea carcumber drove past next to Tom and Jared and they got covered in a thick coating of slime that caused the darkness. Tom noticed the wheel tracks next to them and realised that they could have been crushed. As another car was coming, Tom hoisted himself and Jared into the air when Tom noticed that the slime had got caught in the robot arm and it wasn't moving properly. It had become quieter as fewer cars were driving past so they attempted to try and roll to the other side of the road.

As Tom and Jared were getting across, Harry was practicing walking because he knew he could do it by himself after more practice. It was just easier to travel on the robot arm. Then as he stood up, he tried to walk forward and was able to do it. The rain was stopping so the ground was becoming slippery and wet again but Harry was managing it, until he slipped and fell over. He just needed more practice.

As Tom and Jared were rolling to the other side, they noticed that there was some kind of gutter blocking their way. Almost all of the tar-like slime had been expelled from the robot arm and just as they were about to climb over, they noticed a fish walking her crab along a footpath. Tom and Jared ducked behind the gutter, immediately fell over and decided to play dead. The crab started to wander over to them and sniff their bodies catching the owner's attention. The fish figured that they were road kill as they had tar all over them and didn't seem to be moving.

The fish and the crab walked off, figuring that some humaning-man had thrown them out. The fish turned the corner with the crab and walked to Corals to find something for lunch. Tom and Jared climbed over the gutter and back onto the robot arm to head for the seaweed when they heard Harry yelling. Tom had almost forgotten about him and realised that he would have to cross over the road two more times before they moved on, Jared started to slip and soon fell over as Tom went to run across the road to help Harry.

The World Above
New Frontier
Chapter 13
Conveyor Belts

Meanwhile…

Back in the human trawling boat, Darian, Kelly and Amilia
were getting a little scared from hearing hundreds of people
around them suffer and die. Then when Darian turned back,
she noticed some people had their heads caught in the net
chocking to death. She immediately turned back forward
when the conveyor belt started to slant upwards. As they
looked forward, they saw some sort of metal box everyone
was pulled into. Kelly realised this wasn't good and tried to
pull Darian and Amilia along to get away when a heap of
people crashed into them, sending them into the metal box.

They felt ice cold and as Darian, Kelly and Amilia tried to
stay together through the darkness of the metal box. They
heard all kinds of machinery that were spraying everyone with
something, causing everyone to start freezing to death if they
hadn't already drowned. Then as a bright light appeared, they
were shot out of some kind of pipe and landed onto another
conveyor belt.

Amilia almost got sick when she looked around at all the
frozen people around them while Darian and Kelly tried to not
look at them. But their icy bodies were always pressed against
them. Then they saw another conveyor belt with spikes
pointing out of them, bringing up around nine people at a
time.

Kelly didn't know how they could escape and neither did the others, so as they tried to stick together, they let the spikes pull them up. Then when they got to the top, they fell into some tray that they started to slide down. Then when they got to the bottom, they landed on another conveyor belt Everyone was separated from each other a little more now. Then as they were pulled along that conveyor belt, another one appeared with spikes again that would bring them up, but now only taking about 4 at a time. Then as the three of them got into the same one, a fourth person was with them and she stammered, "Ple, ep, e."

Darian didn't like the sight of someone suffering so she spread the shield around her too. Then when they got to the top, they fell and landed on another conveyor belt, keeping them in groups of two to four.

Then as they laid on the conveyor belt, the person they saved was thanking them, but they all knew it wasn't over yet. When they fell off the conveyor belt, they landed into slots. The four of them rolled across the top of the slot and fell backwards with air raining on them and stretching the shield as far as it could go.

Soon after some sliding, they reached a hold up as a bunch of dead bodies was in front of them. Darian was wondering what had stopped them when she saw a giant fish picking up people separately and placing them in separate slots, leading into a machine that sounded like it had brushes and saws.

Darian immediately stood up as Kelly and Amilia followed. The person they rescued followed behind, still gasping for breath and trying to warm up. There was a fish sorting everyone into their slots and another one making sure they were in place properly. The four of them tried to not look down since the sight of dead bodies freaked them out. So they jumped over the bodies, trying not to fall over. The fish that was making sure all the people were in place looked up and gave a bit of a confused look as it saw them running away.

The fish saw Darian, Kelly, Amilia and the other person running away, mentioned it to its partner that it would return soon, and went around to try and grab them.
"Thanks again for saving me, my name is Hayley by the way."
"Cool, thanks for letting us know, now let's move!" yelled Darian. The four of them got to the end of the metal and as they looked around, they noticed there was no way out. Then the fish picked up Darian and Amilia, went around and placed them into separate slots leading into the machine, separating the shield between everyone and making Kelly and Hayley fall over for a breath.

The fish then went back over and tried to look for Kelly and Hayley.
"Mhmm, they all look the same, I can't work out what ones walked, oh well whatever," said the fish. It then went back to work with its partner. Amilia and Darian felt the conveyor belt move as they noticed spinning circles around them. Then Amilia felt the brushes against her as she went into the machine to meet a lot of blades. The spinning circles were spinning around her faster when she looked across and saw a horrifying sight of what was happening to everyone, and that's when she vanished.

Darian realised Amilia went into the machine and as tears formed in her eyes, she got up and felt the brushes against her when she jumped off and landed on the ground. Kelly and Hayley saw what Darian did and blacked out from lack of breath as the fish grabbed the two of them and placed them both in the slots. They were both unconscious and cold with no strength to get away as the conveyor belt sent Kelly through the brushes of the machine. Hayley soon had the brushes slide above her as Kelly was put in place to have blades appear around her. Then as they shot at her, they stopped just inches from her, just before she drowned.

The fish noticed Darian jump down and run away as it decided to chase her. The fish reached down while she was fast walking to keep balance, when the fish just froze. Darian got tired and slipped up when she turned back and noticed the fish wasn't moving anymore. In fact, nothing was moving anymore. Darian wasn't sure how long this would last so she continued running off to hide.

Kelly opened her eyes looking up and across at some blades surrounding her. She got up realising she could stand and walk over to Hayley. Hayley also opened her eyes but she was still shivering from the cold air. Then Kelly noticed nothing was moving and pulled Hayley up to help her. Hayley got up realising they were able to breathe again as they walked over the dead people in front of them and crawled under the brushes. Then they felt the brushes move with them.

They crawled under noticing the brushes moving and then they started to slip. They ran to the side of the conveyor belt noticing the fish moving a little and that's when they both jumped off and hid under it. Then laid low under the conveyor belt while it continued to work again with fish moving around. Then Kelly turned back and saw a puddle of air near them. As they started to struggle in breathing underwater, they placed their faces into the puddle of air to breathe properly again. Safe from the fish that couldn't see them.

Darian also hid away from the fish by hiding under some other kind of machinery. The fish chasing her then started moving around again as if nothing ever happened. The fish looked around and realised it had completely lost Darian. Then it figured that it must have been delusional to think humans could actually walk in the world above. The fish decided to just turn back and get back to work with its partner.

Darian looked around not knowing where to go next while Hayley and Kelly couldn't go anywhere without air to breathe. Then as they realised they weren't going anywhere, they decided to relax. When Darian looked around the corner, she saw Kelly and Hayley knowing that there had to be a way for the three of them to get away. They just weren't sure how yet.

The World Above
New Frontier
Chapter 14
Mind, Body and Soul

In the World Above…

Adam had run across the path holding Josh/Nick, Seth and Rusheel in his massive hands. He ran along the line of shops and noticed a store with a human tank that was much bigger than the one they were in before. They immediately decided that maybe if they snuck in there and took some of the air, they could escape and run back to the others. Adam lowered them to the ground waiting for everyone to jump off. Then when the others were falling over each other, Adam reached up and opened the door a bit, then he reached down to hoist the others in.

Adam lifted the others into the store and he slowly shut the door. Rusheel looked around and noticed a serving counter and the people inside the human tank. They saw an opening that could lead them behind the counter and ran there to hide in case someone walked into the store. While Nick was standing there in Josh's body and was helping him find a way out.

Rusheel had an idea that they could run across the edge of the wall, until he noticed a fish walk into the store. There was another fish working at a cooking stove and was placing something into a fry vat. They didn't really want to know what was in there so they didn't try to think about it that much as it didn't look like chips. As they waited there, Adam

---

noticed another image slowly appear in his head, showing an image of the fish walking out to change the bins and that's when Adam knew how they could get to the human tank.

"So what is your plan to get out of here Josh?" said Nick.
"Well, I figured that you could just leave my body and I'd be set free," said Josh.
"Sorry, but that is a bad plan because where would I go, I'd just be a spirit that would disappear into nothing eventually," replied Nick.
"Well, what else can we do to escape?" asked Josh.
"I could just leave you here and live out my life in your body," said Nick.
"Wait, what, you can't do that to me!"
"Yeah, but I already have."
"No, you can't!"
Then as Josh started to yell at Nick some more, Nick just tuned Josh out of his head as he wasn't a problem to him anymore.

Adam knew that eventually the fish would walk away to take out the trash and the customer would only notice them if they ran across the counter standing straight. As Adam was lifting the others, he noticed that his arms were stretching. Rusheel looked down and noticed that they were higher than usual and were almost able to climb onto the counter, just as the fish turned around to take the trash out.

Rusheel and Seth jumped onto the counter and laid low to not be seen. Nick looked around at the others since he had been focused on Josh for a second and soon jumped onto the counter as well. Seth and Rusheel were definitely sure something was wrong with Josh, but they just couldn't work it out. Adam grabbed the edge of the counter and pulled himself up. When he climbed on top of the counter, the others couldn't be bothered asking how Adam stretched his arms since Adam didn't even know.

The fish was tying up the rubbish bag as Adam got Rusheel, Seth and Josh on top of his hands and all started to duck a little. The customer was reading a magazine that hid them from sight. Adam ran them across the edge of the fry vats. When Rusheel looked down, he saw two battered people in the fry vats with chips in the next one. Although Rusheel was feeling sick, he knew that he just needed to stop thinking about the disturbing sight.

"You're not Josh, are you...Nick?" asked Seth.
"What are you talking about, of course I'm Josh," said Nick.
"Mate, I'm from the future and I've known both you and Josh a lot longer than you've known me. I don't really want to know how, but I just want to know right now where Josh is," said Seth.

And after Seth said all that, Nick knew that he was definitely caught, but he wasn't going to just give up the body. Lately, he'd been feeling crazier than usual, and that's when he said to Seth "I'm starting to, feel a little bit hungry," and then looked closely at Seth who was already realising that Nick was about to become really hungry, and nothing would change that.

Adam made it to the edge of the counter and stretched the others to the one opposite it. Then as everyone climbed off, they fell over straight away. Adam grabbed the side and pulled himself across. As Rusheel watched this happen, he noticed how slow the fish was taking to put out the trash, and when he looked across through the hallway, he noticed the bag floating mid-air while the fish seemed to be frozen in time. He thought it was weird and just decided to ignore it.

"Guys, this isn't Josh, he's been possessed by Nick and we need to get him ou…"
"No, no, no, no, no! Come on Seth, I'm not Nick. How paranoid can you be? Thi, this is just how I act regularly, plus how would you know this. You haven't known me for more than a day."
"Nick, I'm from the future and I have seen and experienced how both of you acted around each other for many years now. If you don't get out, you'll break the time loop and shatter time so you need to get out."

"Mhmm, fine I'll get out if that's what you really want. You'd rather have Josh here than me."
"No, you're needed just as much as Josh is, we'll find somewhere for you to go."
"I know that, I'm just going to try and help out a little, the only way I know how."
As he said that, Nick was beginning to leave Josh's body, so he could show everyone just how needed he was.
The fish had finally finished throwing out the garbage and returned to the fry vats. Then as it turned to the side, everyone realised it had seen them.

Adam had already started to run towards the human tank as everyone was talking above him. The fish had a surprised look on its face from seeing walking humans when Nick said, "Watch this."

Nick had completely floated out of Josh's body as he went to levitate towards the fish, but Josh still wasn't waking up, and possibly never could.

While Nick was gliding towards the fish, Adam was in front of the humaning tank so he started to stretch his arms to the top of it. Rusheel grabbed Josh and threw him over first so he was safe from the fish, and watched as he fell slowly to the bottom. Adam was kind of confused on why he wasn't falling a little faster to the ground like he did in the trench, but figured that the world was still changing including the gravity. As Adam lifted himself up, the other people had already run into their house at the back of the tank, while Rusheel jumped in to make sure Josh was okay.

While Adam was stretching himself up, Nick was haunting the fish by possessing parts of it. He would become its hand and make him slap himself, or fly into the fish's foot and make him step backwards. The fish was freaking out, thinking that his place was haunted, and seeing Adams long arms and giant hands, while standing at the same time blew its mind and caused him to run off. The customer was concerned about it as well and waited outside not really wanting any part of it.

Nick noticed that without a body he would soon vanish from existence and that's when he started to get even hungrier than before. Then he saw the others looking defenceless, making him lose control of his hunger and begin to fly angrily towards Josh's body so that he could live forever. Rusheel and Seth looked up at Nick and noticed that he looked angrier than usual, and then his teeth started to grow uncontrollably fast and sharp. With massive arms full of muscle and pointed fingers, he flew past everyone and straight into Josh's body when Seth realised Nick had turned into one of the hungry-ones.

Josh didn't know what to do in his head. He just sat there thinking about how screwed he was. Then that was when he realised the room was actually getting darker, and he could sense something else with him.

"You've been around for long enough Josh, and when I'm done with you, you will be stuck inside that bubble forever, gone from existence, never to be mentioned again."

Then as Nick said that, a pair of glowing red eyes appeared in front of Josh with a grinning mouth as it started to creep further towards him.

"Why are you doing this mate, I thought you were trying to help us," yelled Josh.

"I was, but then I got betrayed and left behind. I was treated like I was nothing compared to you, but when I'm done, you'll all be nothing.

Josh stepped back further as Nick continued to talk.

"Once I take over your body, I will consume every last bit of you while consuming everyone you know or have seen in this area. It all ends now and there's nothing you can do to stop me!" yelled Nick.

Then as there was nowhere else for him to go, Josh watched as Nick started to consume all parts of his mind and ending with Josh.

Part of Nick was inside Josh while the other part of him left his body looking more demonic and powerful than before. Then as he overlooked everyone, he grew a third arm in his chest and stretched his three arms to grab Seth, Adam and Rusheel. Then without any struggle, Nick started to pull their souls out of their bodies. He was also shrivelling Josh's body at the same time.

First Rusheel's soul came out of him as he started to scream in pain, only to soon disappear into Nick. Then just before he was consumed, he vanished into a blue light with spinning circles around him. Nick wasn't sure what had happened to Rusheel, but didn't care as he continued to consume Adam and Seth's souls, but there was something different about Adams soul. It was darker than all of the others, and that's when Nick realised he'd stuffed up.

"You dare disturb me again you insignificant moron. I already warned you once, and now you will pay," boomed Adams soul. Nick noticed Adams tiny soul in all of the darkness and realised that his arms were slowly darkening like the arm of Adams spirit. Nick immediately let go, but the darkness continued to spread up his arm. Then the spirit reached over, grabbed Nick's other two arms and made him scream in pain. This caused him to let go of Seth's soul just before Seth shrivelled into dust, and allowing Seth to start looking normal again

Nick had spread everywhere within the mind and was starting to consume Josh until Nick backed off and started to scream in pain. The darkness of Adams spirit was spreading across the mental part of Nick too and was weakening him even more. As he got weaker, Josh started to feel more powerful and walked towards Nick's decaying spirit.

When Seth slowly woke up, he noticed the demon creature attacking Nick. Then they saw Josh's body slowly shrivelling up. The demon then grabbed Nick's face, making him fall to the ground in pain, also making Josh's body start to look normal again.

In the mind, Nick was shrinking down and getting weakened. He started to stagger backwards away from Josh as the spirit had taken over him. Then as Nick slowly became Josh's height, Josh walked up to Nick and pushed him against the wall of his mind, and punched him out of it. Then as Nick left his body for good, Josh returned to his normal self and got reanimated into his own body. He woke up, not really understanding how he won the fight until he saw Adam's soul, killing what was left of Nick.

Nick shrunk back into how he originally looked, but curled in a ball. Then as he started to get skinnier, he soon became a skeleton, and eventually disappeared leaving nothing behind. The demon snarled at everyone while saying, "You have all been warned to never disturb me, or else you'll follow Nick into the eternal darkness of the void."

The demon started to float backwards into Adams body and when the demon was hidden from sight, Adam woke up, looking around and wondering if he'd missed anything as the others hiding in the house were wondering what had just happened.

Seth walked over to them while Josh and Adam were still trying to catch their breath. Then as Seth looked around, he realised Rusheel wasn't around anymore.
"Guys, did anyone see where Rusheel went? Seriously, where is Rusheel? We need to find him."
Seth immediately ran over to the others hiding away while Josh was helping Adam up.

"Guys, did any of you see what happened to the other guy that was with us? Where did he go?"

"I…I don't know where that guy went, he kind of just shrivelled up into nothing and vanished into a blue light," said one of the guys.

"This is not good, not good at all, everything is over now. The future cannot happen anymore."

"What are you talking about, I'm sure the future will be fine."

"No, it won't be fine. Now everything is over. I have failed," said Seth.

The guy Seth spoke to had become curious about what was going on so he stayed with Seth and said, "Look, my names Mitchel and I don't really know what to say right now. All that I can think of is that you're trying to get over the death of your friend, but I'm sure everything will soon be fine. Kai and I have been fine so far haven't we."

"I don't care, just get away from those guys before they do something crazy again," said Kai.

"Okay then, I better go now… and maybe you guys should go soon too."

Seth understood why they didn't want them to be around so he walked off as Josh walked over to Mitchel and Kai to quickly ask, "Hey, um, I've only just started thinking about this, but how did you guys end up in a human tank so quickly?"

"What do you mean 'quickly', I got captured a month ago and have been living in this twisted world for six months now. Don't ask Kai this question though he'll say he'd been living in this tank for eight months and been living in this world for three years. How long did you think we had to get in here?" asked Mitchel.

"Um, I'm pretty sure the world has only been like this for a couple of days now," stammered Josh.

"That can't be right, I've lived every moment of this world and it's been around for about three years now. You know what, you guys are really weird, maybe you should all go," snapped Kai.

Josh immediately stood up to get away and started to walk off to catch up to Seth and Adam. As Seth was walking, he realised something. Time hadn't shattered yet. Maybe everything was fine and that somehow Rusheel and Nick would return, he just wasn't sure how that could happen.

The World Above
New Frontier
Chapter 15
The Void

Nick opened his eyes and was surprised to see that he could still see things. All around him he saw creatures and aliens not moving and just floating around. He wasn't sure what would happen to him in the void, but he knew it wouldn't be good. He remembered reading a book about this place before. The character in the book was kind of in the same position he was in. Once the darkness consumed you, you would go through the stages of an eternal death.

First, he would lose his five senses and every positive emotion in him.
Next, all muscle movement would be disabled in his body including blinking.
Third, he would lose every memory he ever had including how to talk.
Then, everyone outside the void would forget his entire existence, so no one could ever think of him.
And finally, he would become immortal, so he'd have to deal with all the pain for eternity, fading into the darkness, never to be heard of again, with no way to reverse the effect, and no way of ever getting out.

Then as Nick looked around him, he noticed the darkness spreading towards him, causing him to start losing his vision a little and realised he needed to get out of there fast. He flew away from the spreading darkness and saw how everyone else was. They weren't moving any part of their body and their eyes were destroyed because they probably forgot how to blink. They were all breathing, but looked very sad. He floated past all of them and soon saw his lifeless body floating in the darkness. He looked up and saw the vortex that he'd originally escaped from as well.

He flew over to his body and all he could see of it was his arm. He immediately grabbed it and tried to pull it out of the darkness. Then once he got his whole body out, he started to fly to the vortex. As he was getting closer to the vortex, the darkness was creeping up on him and was gradually becoming part of him. Then as his spirit combined with his body again, he reached his hand into the vortex as the darkness was smothering his legs. He started to feel weaker and as his hand was sliding out, he felt someone grab his hand and pull him back in.

Even though Nick was inside the vortex, the darkness was still weakening it and was gradually trying to smother everyone in it. Nick felt a huge surge of pain as he got pulled into the vortex and was reluctant that his legs were healing as they weren't in the darkness for too long. He noticed these blue spirit-like beings look him over and before he knew it, one grabbed his arm. Nick noticed Jacob's, Scott's and Teresa's faces inside the spirits arm and as he was about to become like them, the spirits talked in some ghostly language.

Nick was looking around, not knowing what his fate would be when he noticed the darkness appearing inside the vortex behind them and start to spread closer. The spirits noticed it and immediately created a rift, allowing another vortex to appear as they sent Nick into it. Nick was thrown into it and started seeing lights flash around everywhere.

Then when he looked back, he noticed the ghostly figures fly away very fast down the original vortex. Then the darkness smothered that vortex and continued to chase after Nick. He also noticed dark patches everywhere inside the vortex as it was slowly seeping through. He didn't want to risk flying into it anymore so he tried to glide around it.

The darkness was right behind him, almost touching his feet as Nick had flown to the left and to the right and then down and up, but as the vortex got longer, it also got skinnier, so soon Nick just started to fly into the darkness without control, and the skinnier the vortex got, the more colours Nick saw. The darkness had reached his feet and was stretching up his legs while other parts of the darkness were reaching up his left arm as his right arm was in front of him.

Then as the darkness continued to smother his body he noticed an end to the vortex while the darkness was reaching up his neck and surrounding his head. And as the darkness smothered his head and everything else, his hand remained and touched the end of the vortex.

When he got pulled into it, all he saw was flashing colours around him while in the distance, he noticed the silhouettes of people above him and reached out his hand into their world to call out for help. Then as the darkness was still forming around him, a golden hand appeared from one of the silhouettes within the light of the world he was entering, ready to pull him into an unknown world, where he may never act the same way ever again.

The World Above
New Frontier
Chapter 16
Day at Corals

While Tom was busily crossing the road back and forth to get Harry, and Adam was carrying Rusheel, Seth and Josh, Ben made sure everyone stuck close to him, making sure they didn't break the shield that was helping them breathe. Regen, Bailey and Ben hurried along a footpath and hid behind a bin, just as a bunch of fish were walking past and not noticing them.

Regen looked closely at the door and noticed it was one of the automatic doors that opened when someone walked near it. They were prepared to run in until they realised how busy it was and that they'd been lucky to have even made it to the bin. One after the other, fish walked by and he realised that they could never get in. One of the fish walked out with an air Popsicle and walked near the bin. Regen got everyone to play dead and as the fish looked at them, it was just grossed out by the look of them and walked off.

Ben and Bailey were standing back up when they looked at the path and saw the fish run over to another fish in a uniform. Ben couldn't really work out what it was saying until the fish pointed at the bin and the uniformed fish put on a glove and walked towards it. The fish had told the uniformed fish to dispose of them. Regen got up, realising that he was kind of getting hungry. He ignored it, knowing that he'd be able eat soon. Then he heard Ben and Bailey telling him to hurry as they needed to run close together.

They ran to an automatic sliding door to realise they weren't noticed by the sensor. They tried to pry it open with their hands when Ben realised that this may have been one of those doors where you could only exit from it. And that there was another one up ahead. The uniformed fish was quite surprised that the humans were walking around, but still wanted to catch them. It bent down to grab them as Bailey got the others to start running towards the other sliding door.
The fish was jogging behind them since watching the humans run was kind of funny for the fish. As Ben and the others were running, the fish was behind them being quite interested in what they were doing. Regen ran up front and as they realised this door wasn't opening, the door sensed that the fish was there and opened to let them through. They were all trying to stay close together as they didn't want to risk breaking the shield.

They looked around and saw a bunch of trollies lined up behind one another and ran in that direction. Then before the fish knew it, the humans ran under the trollies and knew that it needed to get serious about catching these humans or else they'd soon get free. The fish reached into his pocket and grabbed out a key to pull out each trolley. Then he unlocked each individual trolley and pulled each of them out.

Ben and Bailey were ducking under the trollies up front while Regen was behind and getting noticed by the fish every time it pulled out a trolley. The fish had pulled out around eight trollies as they managed to get to the end of it. Then as they saw a way to escape, they noticed that no more trollies were getting pulled out anymore. They thought they were safe because the fish seemed to be looking away from them at the mess it had created. Then in frustration, the fish reached forward to grab the remaining two trollies at once and pulled them out, making a metal part of the trolley hit Regen over the head.

Regen felt a little dazed and confused, and as he stood up, he felt Bailey grabbing his arm and pulling him along through the gap in the trolley aisle. As the fish saw them escaping, another fish walked up to him and asked why he pulled out all of the trollies. Bailey turned back and had trouble understanding what the fish were talking about until the fish walked away, leaving the uniformed fish placing the trollies back where they were before.

Regen feeling dizzy, started to walk around in circles when he realised they were running past a butcher section. While the others were looking away from it in disgust, Regen looked at it hungrily and drooled over it, especially when they reached the air food section. Regen reached into his pocket to grab an air mask as he immediately ran towards the air food section, pulling the others with him. Bailey fell over, pulling Ben over as Regen also fell.

His eyes appeared bloodshot as veins were bulging up his arms. There were no fish wandering around this area as Regen had a grin on his face while looking at the others. Regen appeared to look stronger and he was drooling just looking at the others.

"I'm very hungry," said Regen. Then as he started to bend over, his nails grew pointier. Then as he was about to leap at them, Ben deactivated the shield, grabbed Bailey and reactivated it around him.

Regen immediately fell over as he was struggling to breathe, when he placed the air mask on his face to breathe properly. Ben immediately got Bailey to start running as they headed off to the shelves full of food. Regen however constantly fell over as he tried to wobble over to the others. A fish had noticed this and walked up behind Regen to pick him up, until he showed off his sharp teeth making the fish back off from him.

The fish immediately kicked him away and Regen went sliding across the ground towards the others climbing the shelf. Ben and Bailey were climbing up when Regen came sliding behind and managed to grab Bailey's foot. Bailey was hanging onto the shelf as Ben climbed up and started to help Bailey up as well, while Regen was hanging onto his leg. As they ran through the shelf, they were pushing items off, causing a scene for the fish to see.

As items got pushed off the shelves, more fish appeared to see what was going on. Soon someone with gloves and a net appeared and reached down to grab the humans. Regen was desperately trying to bite Bailey's leg as it looked so juicy and delicious from his point of view. Regen's strength had increased and wasn't letting go when spinning circles started to form around him. The fish moved some items away as he set the net to grab the humans as the other fish watched in shock.

More spinning circles appeared around Regen and then out of nowhere, Ben and Bailey got pushed into the net just as Regen broke part of the shield, making it deactivate. Then just as Regen opened his mouth as wide as possible, he leaped at Bailey as the spinning circles surrounded Regen more and made him vanish into the blue light. The fish hoisted the two of them into the air and carried them to the butcher area to place them somewhere else.

They looked around, not knowing what would happen to them as they got dropped into some sort of milk container. Ben got up cautiously so that he didn't trap his foot in part of the container. He turned around making sure Bailey was close by, but slipped up on one of the gaps. This was a weird type of container, but also looked kind of familiar. Bailey got up tried to slip through one of the gaps in the side of the container, but couldn't fit through them.

As Ben reactivated the shield around himself and Bailey, they heard the fish that captured them talking to something that looked like a phone.
"No, I'm not joking around right now. I'm serious, I saw humans running across the supermarket floor.
No, I'm not kidding, seriously, I have the humans in a container.
Just come down here and I'll show you them.
Oh come on, you can't say your too busy to see humans that can walk around in a supermarket alive.
No, I can't just bring them to you, they… they need to be studied, analysed, dissected. I'm going to be famous for finding these humans.
No, don't say I'm overreacting. I'm underreacting. I mean, I also saw a human vanish in a blue light.
Ok, ok, just come and see them, you won't regret it."

Bailey and Ben couldn't hear much of the conversation the fish was almost yelling, but now they were concerned about one of the things it said.

They need to be studied, analysed, and dissected.
Then once the fish was done talking on the phone, it turned back to the humans and looked them over once more and realised they were still standing and not falling over like they should have been. Then the fish pulled out a camera and took a picture of them standing.

When the fish put the camera away, it heard a bell ring and went to the counter to serve a customer. Bailey knew that this was their chance to escape as he noticed they'd be able to climb out so he started to climb up the gaps of the container and signalled Ben to follow as well.

During all of this though, Ben continued to question if the fish acted as enemies in this adventure. He understood that most of them wanted the humans dead, but there was that one fish that helped them escape the house in the beginning. That didn't matter though since the majority of the fish didn't like humans, so they were definitely classed as the villains.

Ben and Bailey had to all climb over at the same time to prevent the shield from stretching too much as the two of them jumped down and ran behind the container to be kind of hidden from the fish. As they ran behind the container, they noticed a sink, realised they were placed on a bench, and ran to the edge of the sink so they could slide down the exposed pipe.

They tried to slide down as close together as they could and when they landed, they immediately ran under the table when the customer the fish was talking to, noticed the humans were running around. The fish immediately turned around to see what was happening when it saw the humans running under the table and immediately face palmed itself as it should have known they'd be able to climb out if they were able to stand.

The fish immediately bent down to reach for Bailey as they both ran under the empty cardboard boxes to hide. The fish looked through all of the boxes to try and find the humans when it noticed the two of them running off. The fish knew that they couldn't run fast enough to escape, but as it reached down to the humans, they started to vanish away from him.

Ben figured that they wouldn't be able to run away until he noticed the fish completely stop moving. He asked Bailey what was going on and he wasn't sure either. They just figured this was a chance for them to escape so they just ran off. As they ran across the floor, a blue aura started to surround Ben as he watched Bailey freeze in time. Then as Ben looked around at his surroundings, he noticed Beth standing next to him.

"Hey, welcome to the time roommate. This is a world between worlds, a place within the most hidden places in time and space. Mhmm, this room is actually pretty neat. Just don't move around too much or else you'll be sent to the void… anyway, I just thought I should drop in for a bit and give you some advice," said Beth.
"Um sure. Wait. Did you say I'm in a time room and that I could be sent into the void?"

"Yes, don't worry about that too much just yet though. You'll know all about it soon. I only did this because I didn't want him over there seeing it yet."

"Who, Bailey? Why?"

"I don't know, no reason. Anyway, I thought I should just tell you to go to the second shopping cart over there if you want some food."

"Ah okay, thanks, I'll make sure I go there."

"Nice. Alright, I'm going to head off now so see ya. Oh and by the way, no one else you know, knows about this place. So don't mention it to anyone. See ya later."

Then as Ben appeared back in reality, Bailey started to move again as Ben stated that they should go to the second shopping cart at the second conveyor belt. Bailey didn't know why, but he went there anyway.

They tried to stay as hidden as possible to try not to draw too much attention to them as they ran when Ben noticed the fish still not moving for some reason. In fact, everyone in the entire store seemed to just freeze in time. They both saw this as a chance for them to run to the second trolley as it appeared to have food in it. The fish that was with the trolley seemed to be completely frozen in time as Bailey and Ben climbed up it and noticed a packet of human food on the conveyor belt.

The checkout fish was also frozen in time as Bailey and Ben ran across the conveyor belt. They jumped over a couple of groceries when the conveyor belt started to move. Then all of the fish in the store started to move again as both of them fell over on the conveyor belt. Then as the checkout fish moved normally again, it picked up the human food, only to drop it and stare in awe at the humans that started to stand up. Then the fish buying the groceries noticed the humans and tried to pull the groceries away from them. That was when the fish chasing them started to move normally and frantically tried to find them.

Bailey and Ben got up as they ran under the scanner, picked up the human food and jumped down as they knocked over the groceries in the plastic bags. Both of them threw the food in front of them and frantically crawled over the plastic bags when they soon jumped down, picked up the food, and ran to the exit. The deli fish ran to the checkout with the massive mess, and noticed the two humans running away with the food.

Then as it was about to chase them, another fish walked up from behind and wanted it to help clean up the grocery mess, and because it wasn't in a position to say no, it decided to leave the walking humans and not bother them… unless he had the chance to properly expose them to the world since everyone needed to know about this.

The World Above
New Frontier
Chapter 17
Hunger

Ben and Bailey immediately made a run for the road so that they could meet up with the others. They ran across the field, got to a footpath and saw Tom with Harry still crossing the road. Bailey wasn't sure why they were still there until they looked closer to the edge of the road and saw Jared shaking much like how Regen was before he turned into a cannibal.

Jared was staring at Tom hungrily. Not Harry though since he looked gross to eat and was made up of fish shaped plastics. Then he realised Ben and Bailey were nearby. As Jared turned around, Bailey and Ben were beginning to step back. Then when Jared realised they were near him, he started to grin, showing his sharp teeth. He realised that Tom would be difficult to eat because of the robot arm, and ran across the dried up land towards them, ferociously with bloodshot eyes.

Bailey and Ben immediately turned around as they ran backwards, throwing the food away so they could run faster. Jared saw the food get thrown away and immediately drew his attention to that as the others got further away.
"Be careful guys, that's still Jared that's standing in front of us. Remember he isn't in control so we shouldn't harm him," said Bailey.
"No, I'm fine. I'm, just, really… hungry!!!!" yelled Jared.
Then, as he walked over to Ben and Bailey he started to grin.

"Something must have infected him, don't let him bite you!" yelled Bailey.

"I'm no zombie, I'm just really, really, hungry!" yelled Jared.

Ben and Bailey turned and looked at each other when Jared chased after them, thinking that they would taste better than the packaged human food. The two of them couldn't split up and the water was slowing them down. Then Bailey tripped up on something and pulled Ben down as well. Jared walked up to the two of them as he opened up his mouth, grabbed Ben's head and pulled him upwards, preparing to rip his head off.

Jared was also standing on Bailey so he couldn't get up. Then when Jared pulled off his air mask, Bailey reached up, grabbed Jared's arm, and pulled it down. As Jared started to drown, Bailey knocked the air mask out of his hand and trapped his legs. Jared angrily shook Bailey's hands off and scratch his arm, making Ben punch Jared in the jaw, causing them both to stagger backwards. Jared's nose started to bleed as he slipped closer towards Ben.

Ben noticed blue spinning circles surrounding Jared as he tried to get away from them, but they just followed Jared anyway. Then in a final attempt of hunger and desperation, he immediately ran as fast as he could at Ben, mouth open wide and leaped through the air.

Bailey ran at Ben to push him as Jared was mid-air and noticed he was turning blue and disappearing. Then as Jared scratched Bens arm and Bailey's face, Jared was just about to bite down on Bailey's head until he vanished into the blue spinning circles leaving no traces of him being around.

Tom had finally managed to get Harry across the road when they noticed Bailey and Ben on the ground bleeding. As Tom got to Ben to see what happened, Harry noticed the human food nearby and knew they needed to get it before a fish found it. Ben was confused by a few things though and he knew he needed to ask Seth the question.

If the shield protected him against lava back when he was in the trench a while ago, why didn't the shield prevent Bailey and himself from being scratched? At first, he was confused on how Jared was able to walk as well, but then he figured the rain dried up the ground enough for him to walk.

The rain had stopped when Tom went to grab the food and hide in some kind of long seaweed. This was so that the fish wandering past didn't notice they were there. Bailey opened up the packet of human food so that each of them could eat a little as they were getting somewhat hungry and didn't want to end up like Jared.

"Hey guys, what happened to Regen?" asked Harry.

The World Above
New Frontier
Chapter 18
Flight of the Hungry-Ones

Back in the World Below

Kate, Michaela and Tara boarded the plane willingly as they followed Ben. Tara wandered down the aisle with the others looking for a seat, as there were quite a few people on the plane. Kate and Michaela found a seat next to each other and Tara decided to sit behind them.

Ben walked down the aisle and sat next to Tara. As everyone put their seatbelts on, Kate noticed other people outside the plane and told Michaela. They both looked out and realised that two of the people outside had become hungry-ones and both slaughtered someone near them. Then afterward, they picked up heavy tools and placed them in their pants pockets to use later as they started to walk closer to the plane. Then when the hungry-ones noticed the plane was moving, they knew that there were people in there and suddenly got even hungrier.

The plane turned and started to go down the runway as the hungry-ones started to chase the back of the plane. Kate immediately turned around to tell Tara and Ben about the hungry-ones, but although they were a little worried about them, they tried not to think about it too much as there was nothing they could really do about it. Then as Ben sat back on his chair, he noticed blue circles appear nearby which got him curious. Then as the blue circles got brighter, someone appeared behind him and Tara. Ben turned back and noticed Bailey behind him wanting a chat with Ben.

The plane had sped up and was preparing lift off as the hungry-ones were chasing after it. Then with one final jump, they leaped onto the back of the plane to start the hunt. The two of them climbed all over the plane as it took lift off and flew into the clouds.

"What, how did you get here, I-I thought you, you...."
"Died Ben, yeah that's what I thought happened too, but for some reason, I ended up here," whispered Bailey.

Then Tara looked around and whispered to Ben, "I don't know what you're talking about right now, but I'm sure it's about the hungry-ones right?"
"No, why?" asked Bailey.
"Because there is one of them on the wing of the plane," answered Tara.
Then as they all looked out the window, they saw them on the wing pulling panels off and ripping apart electrical equipment.
"I still don't understand how though Bailey, I watched you drown, there's no way you could have ended up here."
"Don't worry about it now, we just need to find a way to get to the hungry-ones and stop them," said Bailey.
"I don't know what you're talking about, but do we still have the guns from the car?" asked Michaela.
"Yeah, I have four bullets in one, why?" asked Tara.
Then Kate turned around and yelled, "There's smoke coming out of the wing!"

The two hungry-ones scattered all over the plane trying to find a way to get in. They knew that bringing down the plane would kill them, but they didn't care, they were just really hungry.

As one of the hungry-ones carefully climbed onto one wing, the other one climbed onto the other. They figured that if they were caught trying to damage the wing, many people would appear at the windows to find them, and that's when the hungry-ones would get them.

Tara then pulled out her gun and aimed it at the hungry-one on the wing of the plane as everyone around stayed away. The wing was smoking up, but the hungry-ones weren't in sight anymore. Then other people on the other side pointed out that the other wing was smoking up and everyone ran to that side as well. Tara aimed the gun at the window with no one paying attention to it since no one could work out what caused the smoke. Then suddenly, everyone heard one of the windows being smashed as a hammer was slashed against it multiple times. Followed by an arm flying through it, grabbing someone screaming for help as everyone turned to that direction.

A hand had reached through the window, grabbed someone by the collar and had pulled their head out the window. Then as the person screamed for help, everyone was pulling him back when another tool smashed the window with someone else getting pulled out of it. Most of the people stepped back in fright when the wall was getting pulled out and one of the hungry-ones gnawed through one of the guy's necks, making him turn limp. Then the other hungry-one bit through the other guys' neck as he turned limp.

"Everyone, stay away from the windows!" yelled Tara.

The hungry-ones hadn't damaged the wings of the plane too badly, but they were trying to get through the walls of the plane.

Then as everyone was staying away from the walls, an ear piercing scream occurred as a flight attendant stumbled out of the toilets, holding a bloody hand. Then after dropping it, people realised the hand belonged to the person who was in the cubicle. The door to the toilet fell to the ground as the flight attendant walked over to everyone with blood dripping down her grin, preparing to feast.

The World Above
New Frontier
Chapter 19
The Final Bullet

Everyone stayed as far back as they possibly could from the cannibal flight attendant when Tara pushed in front with the gun in her hand getting ready to fire. They all stayed still when the hungry-ones on the sides started to smash holes in the plane, making people get flown over the seats and into the clutches of the hungry-ones who immediately ripped at their necks. Tara stayed standing being swayed from side to side as those alive fell to the ground.

People were getting slaughtered all over. Kate and Michaela fell over and were getting pushed against some chairs. Bailey was also getting pushed against some of the chairs when Ben got blown off his feet and landed on someone against the wall. Tara was struggling to stand straight as she was hearing cries pain around her.
Then as the hungry-one was preparing to run down the aisle towards her, Tara fired a bullet. The bullet flew through the air as someone fell in front of the hungry-one, causing the bullet to fly through her head as she collapsed to the ground.

Tara thought she shot the hungry-one until she realised the hungry-one was still standing. Then the flight attendant bent over and gnawed at the dead person's neck, and Tara realised in shock, that she had shot an innocent person that must have fallen in the way. Then the hungry-one stood straight and walked over to everyone when Tara dropped the gun, realising just how dangerous the weapon was, making the hungry-one step towards her victoriously.

Michaela was holding on to a chair as she was close to the hole in the plane that was causing people to be blown out of it. Kate kept balance and noticed Tara fall to the ground in regret as the hungry-one proceeded towards her. Then as the gun fell near Kate, she knew what she had to do. She aimed the gun at the hungry-one and was about to fire it, until she had a cleaner idea and shot the bullet through one of the windows.

The hungry-one was just about to grab Tara, when a bullet flew past them, smashed through a window and caused the hungry-one to be blown into it, away from Tara. The flight attendant was stuck at the window, but as she rolled around, she was slowly able to push herself away from it. Then as the cannibal flight attendant was freeing herself, she was reaching to bite Michaela, when instinct kicked in, and Kate fired the bullet.

The bullet flew through the jaw of the flight attendant, as it opened its mouth to bite into Michaela, making it fall on its face and get dragged back to the window.

Ben was struggling to get in front of the chairs when the side of the plane was cracking up. He rolled off the person when one of the hungry-ones grabbed him by the shoulder. Bailey saw this happening and went to help Ben out. He reached from behind the chair, grabbed Ben, and pulled him further away from a hungry-one reaching to bite him. Then when Ben was pulled a good distance away, Bailey started to slip out of his seat.

"Kate, make sure the pilot continues to fly the plane!" yelled Michaela.

"Okay!" yelled Kate.

Kate was still trying to come to terms with what she had now done. She had killed someone, and it didn't seem wrong anymore. It almost felt, normal. Now Kate understood what Michaela had said a while ago. She had to adapt in order to survive, and accept that death was becoming a normal thing.

Bailey was struggling to pull himself off the chairs, as he noticed Ben and attempted to pull himself away from the wall. Ben was getting scratched all over by the hungry-ones until it slipped and fell over. The air rushing out of the plane was making it difficult for anyone to get anywhere, but they were managing anyway.

Tara was getting pushed against the chairs by the wind, but when she saw Ben and Bailey heading off in some direction, she knew to follow.

All they heard around them were screams of pain as they crawled through the aisle of the plane. Then as they looked ahead, they noticed Kate and Michaela not far ahead of them and followed from behind. Some of the survivors on the plane had the same idea, but the entire trip up there was disturbing because of all the dead bodies around. As they got closer to the door, Bailey turned back and noticed the hungry-ones on both sides were creating big enough holes for them to crawl through, and that just made everyone want to hurry up.

Although most people were surprised that the plane wasn't going down, they were glad it stayed in the air. Kate made it to the pilots up front as Michaela appeared from behind and

yelled, "We have to land this plane now before it crashes!"
The pilots knew the wings were smoking up, and had already
started to prepare for the landing, when one of them turned to
them and yelled, "Landing doesn't matter, because at least I'll
die knowing that I had a good feast." Then the pilot leaped out
of the chair at Kate.

The other pilot freaked out as he tried to stay away from the
co-piolet, making the plane go downwards, causing everyone
to fall over. Then as the pilot was crazily trying to slaughter
Kate, she held him back in shock as he was thrown into the
windscreen of the plane. The pilot was trying to push himself
off the windscreen and was reaching for Kate with his arms
outstretched. Then as he showed a menacing grin and
prepared to jump at her, Kate grabbed out the gun, managed to
aim the final bullet at him, stood still, breathed in, and said,
"Welcome to the New Frontier," and fired the bullet straight
through his forehead.

As Michaela ran past Kate, she went to pull the wheel up and
made the plane swoop and fly higher into the sky.
"He had tried to eat you, and he would've eaten me!" yelled
the pilot as he was trying to understand what had just
happened. The plane was still heading up, making the
passengers fall backwards including Tara and Bailey. Then
without warning, they had flown the plane into The World
Above.
Water immediately flooded the plane and as it was about to go
down, Bailey noticed a whole heap of rubbish up there and
had an idea.

"Let's find a way out of the plane and jump onto the rubbish,"
yelled Bailey.

He immediately ran down the plane, followed by Michaela and Ben as the pilot had no other ideas on escaping, except for just landing the plane. They all ran down to the back where they noticed two hungry-ones climbing right into the plane with blood all over them. The pilot wanted to get out of The World Above so he made the plane go down, sending all of the hungry-ones down the plane. As they all ran down the plane, the hungry-ones tripped up on something which sent them to the floor.

Then when they got up, the hungry-ones noticed all the other people on the plane and jumped onto them while Tara got up and followed Bailey down the back. Michaela got up and followed them, but as Kate and Ben were getting back on their feet, one of the hungry-ones saw them, and ran at them when Ben upper cupped it up the jaw sending it backwards and sprawled on the ground. As the five of them ran down to the back of the plane, one of the hungry-ones had had enough with all the trouble and decided that its last feast would be on the pilot.

Bailey looked down and saw a plastic bag beneath them and knew what they needed to do as he jumped out of the plane. The others looked at each other in confusion when they saw him land on the floating plastic bag that allowed him to land on the ground safely. Then they heard the cry of the pilot screaming for help and that was when the hungry-one looked at them and said, "If we're going down, you're going down with us."

The plane immediately started to drift downwards, just as Tara and Ben leaped out of the plane, as there were more plastic bags around for them to land on and float to the ground. Then Michaela and Kate turned to each other, saw the hungry-ones running after them, and jumped out of the plane with one of the hungry-ones following behind them. As they fell, they noticed some kind of milk carton floating around with some other bits of rubbish as well.

The hungry-one frantically tried to reach them, but missed. Kate and Michaela grabbed the plastic and floated to the ground safely. The hungry-one however, fell slower than it probably should have, but when it landed, it didn't get back up again. Then as the five of them immediately ran away from the hungry-one, they saw the plane get caught in all of the rubbish and get pulled to the ground. The aeroplane was completely destroyed at the crash site, and the survival of any other passengers would have been unlikely.

As the group helped each other up, confusion occurred around everyone as no one knew where the rubbish came from, and Ben continued to question Bailey about his death.
"Ben, this is what happened to me just before I drowned. Spinning blue circles appeared around me and I blacked out. Then as I was out, I heard things in the background that mentioned me being an importance in the future. There were other voices speaking about something that may happen soon as well."
"Did you hear what it was?" asked Ben.
"Yes I did, they said something about, 'The war for The World Above'."

The World Above
New Frontier
Chapter 20
Shipped

Within the human trawling ship…
Darian laid low as she hid behind some machinery. She looked back seeing Hayley and Kelly lying flat and keeping their faces in the puddle of air. Darian figured that they weren't going anywhere, but she was also impressed and relieved that they got away. She had to help them, or they'd be soon found. The fish seemed occupied in what they were doing. This didn't mean it would be a walk in the park though. Also, Darian had no idea what else to do and figured they might come up with a plan.

"We're doomed aren't we?" asked Hayley.
"Well unless time freezes again, we can't breathe, or even walk anywhere," answered Kelly.
"Is the puddle of air getting smaller?"
"I think so, we need to take shorter breaths and stop talking, or else we'll drown.
So they just laid there, not talking or doing anything, just thinking and waiting for help. Or death to come to them.

Darian decided she had to move on eventually, so she crawled from her hiding spot and started to speed walk towards Kelly and H- H. She couldn't really remember her name anymore. Darian tried to stay as quiet as possible, but the noise of the conveyor belt and the machine was louder than her anyway.

Darian slowly walked around the legs of the fish. She looked up noticing the fish had their heads down most of the time. Darian wouldn't be able to run straight to them but maybe around them.

Then a thought occurred to her. What the fish were doing to people was a lot like what we did to them. Them seeing a human walking would be weird since for us it would be like seeing a freshly caught fish start walking around. Then she started to think. They shouldn't be trying to kill us. They should be keeping us to find out how we walked. As she paced away from them and started to crawl under the machine, she thought, "Those boneheads killed a walking human. Killed my friend, and they had to pay."

As the fish continued pushing people into their slots leading to slaughter, Darian crawled around wires and pieces of metal until she finally got to Kelly and the other person. Darian wasn't very good with names. She went over, dunked her head into the puddle and when Kelly saw her, she immediately went to hug Darian. She deactivated the shield and reactivated the shield around the three of them. "Sorry, what was your name again?" asked Darian. "Oh, it's Hayley, don't worry about it."

The fish still hadn't noticed them as they continued their job while Darian, Kelly and Hayley continued to crawl out. Then as they passed the wires and pieces of metal, Darian had an idea for revenge. She grabbed the wire and tried to pull it, but her hands kept slipping. Then Hayley asked, "What are you doing with that wire?" Darian answered her and then Hayley said, "Oh, you can use my pocket knife if you want."

Hayley passed it to Darian who opened the knife. Then as Darian tried to cut the wire, Kelly and Hayley just waited. Then when Darian got through half of the wire, Kelly joined her and pulled the wire apart. Electricity sparked shocking Kelly and Darian, causing them to let go. Then they went to another wire and did the same thing, that's when Hayley joined in as well. After tearing two other wires apart, the conveyor belt and all the machinery within it slowed down and soon stopped

The three of them ran along the machine as the fish started to scratch their heads as they wondered what was wrong with the conveyor belt. Darian, Kelly and Hayley looked out from under the machine to see if there were any fish around when they noticed the conveyor belt heading out of the machine. Part of them wanted to see what had happened to everyone that went inside the machinery, but another part of them said to just move on before the fish caught them. Unknown things were happening past that machine, and the three of them figured they'd rather not see it.

They ran away from the conveyor belt and around a corner where they hid behind some boxes. A fish walked down the corridor and didn't notice the three of them hiding there. Then Darian checked the corridor, and signalled for all of them to follow as they ran down it. None of them knew where they were going and then Hayley noticed something from the corner of her eye. Near them was a glowing green square that was slowly spreading across the ground.
"Stop guys, come look at this."
"Look at what?" asked Darian.

Darian and Kelly looked around not finding anything until Hayley pointed to the small green square. They all saw it and weren't sure why it was there. It just seemed too random. Then Kelly noticed that it was spreading and creating more green squares around it. This was near some boxes and as it spread further, it started to spread on the box. The three of them stepped over it and thought it would be best to stay away from that as well. Then as the green squares spread over the box, it spread over most of the floor and gradually got closer to them. Then a fish appeared around the corner, saw them and went to grab them.

As the fish reached down, Darian stepped back and ran away with Kelly and Hayley. Then as the fish was about to catch up to them, it stepped on the green squares. When the fish saw them running away, it stopped chasing them and wondered how they were running.

Hayley looked back to see how far they were when she noticed the green squares spreading across the fish's foot. The green squares spread up to its leg and up its waist, causing the fish to not move properly anymore. Then as it looked down and realised what had happened, the green squares rapidly covered his other leg and both his arms.

Then as it tried to scream out for help, the green squares covered its whole face, leaving it frozen. The squares were spreading slower across the ground, but were still creeping up on Darian, Kelly and Hayley as they started to move further away. Then when the fish was completely covered, little squares collapsed as it started to dissolve into nothing, its fins vanished and so did its fingers and that's when they immediately ran away from it before the squares got them.

The fish started to fall apart as cubic blocks continually dropped off it and disappeared. Then soon its arms were gone and its body had become a stick of glowing cubic blocks. Then as its head fell apart and crumbled, so did its body and it just dissolved into the ground. As Darian, Kelly and Hayley looked back, they noticed in horror that the glowing green squares were spreading towards them. They immediately took off down the corridor away from the glowing squares. Then they noticed two fish walking towards them.

Kelly, Darian and Hayley didn't even really care about the fish anymore as the glowing squares were spreading faster behind them and across the walls. The fish noticed the three of them running and just watched the humans doing something they thought was impossible. Then as they ran past the fish, the fish turned back and watched them running. They tried to follow the humans, but realised that they couldn't move anymore since glowing green squares continued to spread up their legs.

Kelly was up front while Hayley was close behind with Darian following. The glowing squares were speeding faster, catching up to them while the two fish behind had the glowing squares spreading over their faces leaving them frozen and blocky. They reached the end of the corridor and wondered whether they should turn left or right. At first, they weren't sure where to go. Then they saw more glowing green squares coming from the left corridor, just as the two fish fell apart into glowing cubes and dissolved into the ground.

As they ran down the right corridor, they noticed some kind of balcony up ahead of them. The glowing squares had spread past them across the walls and along the floors, allowing it to catch up to them. Then Kelly got a speed boost and ran faster, encouraging Hayley and Darian to run faster as well. Soon they reached the railing. They looked down and realised they had no choice, but to jump. Then as the glowing squares were just about to reach them, they leaped off the humaning ship and landed in the ocean… of air.

The World Above
New Frontier
Chapter 21
The Glowing Cubes

Although they thought they'd just die when hitting the ground, they actually fell kind of slowly flailing their arms everywhere. They landed hard enough to get some bruises, but no serious injuries. It confused them on what happened to their world, but they figured anything could happen in this new frontier.

Then they got up and just looked around, wondering what to do next. Soon Kelly looked up and saw the ship slowly cruising above them. She looked back to see Darian wave her on to follow her and Hayley. They were back to the city to find other survivors because they really had no idea what would happen next.

They started to walk across a bridge that was littered with dead bodies and abandoned cars that were overturned or hanging off the bridge. As they explored the area, they saw human heads around too as they were probably sliced off from the net. Then a car started to slide off the bridge and everyone turned to look as it fell and crashed. Hayley gained an idea to just drive off in one of the cars, which Darian and Kelly agreed with.

They separated to look through cars that still seemed drivable, but that was quite difficult as most cars were total wrecks. Then when Darian looked down the road, she saw a person's arm moving. She decided to run over and help the person, but when she got closer, she saw something familiar. The person that was laying there looked really distressed, and as he reached out his arm and stammered, "Help me," Darian noticed the glowing green squares spreading across his body and up his arm.

As Darian stepped back, she saw the glowing green squares all around him spreading across cars. Then the squares completely covered the guy's arm and face, turning him blocky and crumbled into the ground where he vanished. Darian immediately yelled out to Kelly and Hayley that there were more green squares ahead of them, so they all looked up and ran away.

The glowing green squares were spreading faster behind them, spreading over anything in its path and turning it blocky. Darian, Kelly and Hayley ran along the road noticing the squares spreading along both sides of them. Then they saw a car driving at them. They weren't sure whether to keep running towards the approaching car, but also didn't want to end up turning blocky either. As the car was about to hit the three of them, it braked suddenly, spun to the side and stopped sideways in front of them. Then the window got rolled down and the guy in the car yelled, "Jump in if you want to exist!"

Darian, Kelly and Hayley immediately jumped into the car because they had no other choice, just before the glowing squares reached them. The guy swiftly drove off away from the squares. They thought they were safe from the squares when the driver noticed more patches of the green squares in front of them. The driver did crazy skid turns around the glowing squares. Then just when the driver was approaching the bridge, more green squares appeared blocking their path.

The driver immediately turned to the right and drove up the side barrier of the bridge, keeping the car further off the road and drove over another car, propelling it over the glowing squares and safely over the bridge. Hayley looked back to see if the glowing squares were still following them and was relieved to see that they weren't spreading towards them quickly enough, and disappeared from sight. Darian looked over at the driver, wondering why he had come to rescue them. Then she saw his arm and realised it was robotic. The guy looked over at them and said, "No need for you all to thank me for saving all of you, it was my pleasure."

"Cool. Thanks. But why did you come to rescue us?" asked Darian.
"It was something I had to do and complete. All you need to know is that I know where there is… is… a safe place for us to go, away from any dangers."
"Where's the safe space?
"Somewhere near New South Wales, Australia."
Darian, Kelly and Hayley didn't think it was worth trying to get away since blue spinning circles appeared around their heads, but were curious about one other thing.

"Do you know anything about the glowing green squares that we escaped from?" asked Darian.
"Yeah I do know a little about them, but they're really hard to explain so you may not understand it well."
"Okay, then do the best you can because this seems like something we should know about," said Kelly.

"Alright, I'll tell you about them, and they're not just glowing green squares that makes things blocky. They're something I call 'Time-Correction-Squares', and they're spreading into the past, rewriting history."

Darian, Kelly and Hayley weren't sure what to think about this information, but continued to listen.
"This occurrence isn't just part of our present and becoming our future; it's also becoming the past as well. And if anyone is caught in Time-Correction-Squares, they'll be sent back in time depending on how far it's spread into the past."
"That doesn't make any sense at all. I still have memories of the past and that was before this occurrence happened," said Hayley.

"No, you only remember what you've learnt or experienced and this works the same way, I'll just give all of you an example.
"Imagine that Time-Correction-Squares have spread two years into the past and you touch them at that time. You'll be sent into a different timeline that's connected to ours. Sorry if that made things more confusing, but hear me out. You'd be sent two years into the past without realising anything had happened. That will also be the day you'll believe this occurrence began. If you manage to survive the two years, you'll automatically be joined back into our timeline without realising it and you'll believe this had been happening for over two years, while other people will believe it had only been around for about a week."

"I've met a few people that have been arguing about when this occurrence began because of the Time-Correction-Squares. But they're much worse than that. If the person that was sent back in time doesn't meet up with the original group, or dies before meeting them before the two years are up, the version of you in the original timeline will vanish, either making everyone forget who you are, or making them wonder how you died. And it only gets worse."

"How much worse can it get?" asked Kelly.
"A lot worse, you see this occurrence is spreading through the past, passing your parents, grandparents, great-grandparents and further. If they get sent back in time, something could stop your parents from meeting making you never exist. Same thing for all of your relatives, making you disappear from existence.
There is also a chance that even if your parents do meet and create you, they may do it at a different time or place, making you become a completely different person anyway.
I don't know how to stop Time-Correction-Squares or why they're here, but if we don't find somewhere safe before it spreads past our relatives, we'll disappear from existence."

"Oh and one more thing. Time-Correction-Squares won't stop spreading until they've reached the dawn of time, and when that happens, everyone in existence will be reset making all of us always believe this was how we lived. No one will have any memory of air life living above sea life, and that's when it will be too late fix the world."

"How do we know you're telling the truth," asked Darian.
"You don't. I can't explain this any better than before, but let me ask you all a question.
How long has this occurrence been around for?"
"About a week," answered Darian and Kelly.
"A month," answered Hayley.

The three of them turned to each other in shock, realising that he showed evidence of Time-Correction-Squares affecting people's lives.

Then the driver said one more thing.

"Oh and by the way, my name is Tom and I'm from the future, so I know what I'm talking about."

The World Above
New Frontier
Chapter 22
The Meet up

In the World Above, Seth yelled, "Oh there you guys are!" Immediately everyone turned around to see if he was there with the others. He and Josh were being held by giant hands as Adam carried them over.

"Hey guys. We're back from that human and chips shop by escaping from another human tank," said Josh.

"Oh cool. Wait how did you get out of another Human Tank?" asked Tom.

"The same way we got out of the first human tank, but one of the guys that were already in the tank, Mitchel, helped with getting us out of it afterwards. And we have no idea what's going on with Adam." Stated Seth.

"Hey Tom and Seth, Adam and I have been discussing this for a bit and we were wondering where you were getting these air masks from just in case our ones broke. You were just detaching parts of your robot arm right?" asked Josh.

"I don't know half the things this robot arm can do guys, and I don't take parts of it off to give to you lot anyway, I don't know what you guys saw me do when I got them," said Tom.

"Wait a minute, where did you get all of these air masks from?" asked Bailey.

"A bunch of spinning circles appeared around my arm at the beach and a new compartment with heaps of air masks appeared in it," answered Tom.

"Seth, did you know that there were air masks in the arm?" asked Ben.

"No, I have no idea where they came from," said Seth.

"Guys, who cares about where they came from. It doesn't matter anyway. It's just a good thing we have them," said Ben.

"Did any of you guys bring some air for all of us since these strange air masks have nearly run out of air?" asked Ben.

"Yes we did. Did you bring some food with you?" asked Seth.

"Yes we did," answered Ben.

An awkward silence broke out as Ben finished the conversation and no one really knew what to say.

"Well I hate to interrupt such a conversation right now, but I really have to say this. We are doing so well guys. Seriously it's amazing that we're still around, right Bailey?" asked Tom.

"Yeah, we're doing so… well, heh."

No one understood why Tom and Bailey did that and figured that they were going a little crazy.

"Hey does anyone know how those other guys ended up in the human tank so quickly, acting like they were already used to the new arrangements? This change in the world had only happened for around two days," Ben said.

Josh answered with what Mitchel and Kai told him and no one knew how to process that information except for Seth.

After everyone talked about the possibility of multiple timelines connecting to one big one, Bailey asked, "Wait a minute, why do fish not even know about a difference in the world? Why do they act as if the world has always been like this when we aren't?

"I don't know," stammered Ben.

Everyone one started to fill up their air masks and grab something to eat so that they could prepare for whatever came next.

"Hey Ben, back when we were in the trench a while ago, how did you swim in the lava and survive?" asked Seth.
"I don't know, I guess the shield protected me, and anyway, why weren't you guys burning up standing so close to the lava?"
"I don't know, and I've used that shield before and it was the worst. Couldn't protect me from getting cut by a knife. And you, being in lava which should have burnt you. There is no way we could have survived being any closer to the lava than we were," said Seth.

The other people didn't know what Seth and Ben were talking about, but they did notice the shield was quite useful.
"And how are you getting fresh clean oxygen in your shield all the time anyway, or even keeping it running for so long. It only ever lasted about half a minute for me whenever I used it," yelled Seth.
"You guys, I just want to point out that that's not a shield. It's a force field. You've probably been confusing everyone here by calling it a shield when it's actually a force field!" yelled Tom.
Then Ben yelled, "I will call it whatever I want because its mine anyway.
Then as Ben said that, Seth bent over to him and said, "No, that shield is mine, I'm only letting you use it. I don't know why, but it seems to work better when you have it," said Seth.
"So you're letting me keep it?" asked Ben.
"Mhmm, I guess."

As Seth was done talking to Ben, Seth looked around and realised Regen and Jared weren't there with anyone.

"Um guys, where's Jared and Regen? They both should still be here. Where are they?" asked Seth.

"Oh yeah, um, they both turned into cannibals and disappeared into a blue blur," stammered Bailey.

"We couldn't save them," added Ben.

Seth continued to freak out more since four of the six guys that were supposed to meet in the future had died. He looked around thinking that there was no way he could still be where he was until he realised time still hadn't shattered and everything was fine for some reason. Everyone was disappointed that Nick and Regen didn't make it. But they didn't really know them and Seth shouldn't have been able to know them either.

Then Harry spoke up above everyone and yelled.

"Stop arguing about stuff. It'll all get worked out in the end, and anyway what do we do now guys. Where should we go to get back into our world."

No one really knew how to answer this. They were in the middle of nowhere in a world where everyone wanted to eat or kill them.

Then Tom asked Harry, "Why does part of you look like a weird toy fish?"

The World Above
New Frontier
Chapter 23
The Vision

Ben and Seth had become a little calmer and started talking to each other again. Then Josh went over to talk to them about the experience within his brain. Tom and Bailey were having their own conversation and Harry wasn't really sure why he was with them since he knew no one there and felt like an outsider for looking different from everyone else.

Adam wasn't really in a talkative mood, unlike the others. He kind of just sat somewhere and thought about things. He couldn't work out why everyone had become so afraid of him before. He didn't think some demon had possessed him. He thought it would kind of explain his strange powers, but it really just brought up more possible questions about himself such as the reason why he turned human. Then suddenly Adam felt an image begin to form in his head and decided to work out what it would predict next. It showed three fish wandering past them and heading into a blue sea carcumber. Then the image faded away.

"Hey guys, has anyone else noticed Tom's robot arm appear every so often helping us out through certain situations when he isn't even around?" asked Ben to everyone.
No one really knew what he was talking about and Tom seemed just as confused as them.
"No one knows what I'm talking about then? Never mind."

People like Seth did kind of know what Ben was talking about, but it was just something that happened, and it really could have been anything.

As they were all talking, Ben noticed a blue aura appear around him as everyone froze in time again. But Ben knew where he was.

Beth appeared in the blue aura and asked, "Hey, how's it going? I just thought I should come by again."

"Hey, is it safe for you to be continually freezing time Beth."

"Beth, who's Beth?" But as she said that, she started to twitch a little and soon stated, "Oh right I'm Beth, and yeah it's completely safe… I think. Anyway, I thought I should just tell you that everything Adam says from now on and everything he has said in the past is true, no matter how crazy it sounds."

"Ok, I probably would have believed him anyway before this though. Wait a minute, why did you just twitch a little?"

"I was just a little itchy, and you didn't believe him before. That's why I'm here trying to help you. Anyway, I should probably go now, so, seeya."

"Okay, seeya," and as Ben said that, the blue aura disappeared and everyone continued to move properly again, just as Adam came running over saying he knew where they all had to go to.

Everyone was a little wary of him because of the powers he had, but were ready to listen to what he had to say.

"Okay guys, this may be hard to believe, but occasionally I have visions of the future and they've come true even when I was a cat," said Adam.

No one was really sure what to think of this, and Ben was beginning to notice it as well.

"Okay, so in my vision, I saw three fish walking into a blue seacarcumber."

Everyone was listening and trying to work out what it meant. Then since they didn't really have any other ideas on what to do next, they decided to hear Adam out anyway.

"Do you know where the fish are Adam?" asked Seth.

"I have a small idea of where they are."

Then as Adam said that, he turned and pointed to a blue sea carcumber with three fish wandering out of it.

Then as Seth thought about the situation, he realised that something didn't seem right.

"So what if your vision has started to come true, what does that mean we do?" asked Seth.

"It means they are part of our future and that somehow they must lead us to the right place," answered Adam.

"Wait, that doesn't mean it's part of our future. Maybe yours, but not ours. And what kind of lead is a blue car with three fish in it?" asked Seth.

"What other lead do you have Seth?" asked Adam.

"This one. Instead of your 'vision', I think that we should try to fall down a drain and be soon carried out to the ocean for a safe trip back. Look, there's one just over there by the road that all of us must've not seen."

Then as everyone saw fewer flaws in Seth's plan rather than Adams, Ben realised that he would have followed them as well if Beth didn't show up. He also didn't trust the fish since Adam's plan involved travelling with beings who feasted on people's dead bodies. But Beth was usually right about things so he yelled, "Wait, guys, I think we should listen to Adam."

"Why? The drain is right there. We should be able to get back to our world."

"Look, drains don't lead to the ocean. They lead to DE (Diatomaceous Earth) filtering places where we would get thrown away as trash."

"Mhmm, I guess that sounds about right, but are you sure that'd be more dangerous than driving off with some fish in a world we can't breathe in?"

"Nope, I'm not sure, I've got no idea what's going to happen next, I think that only Adam knows."

"Sorry what, oh right my vision," said Adam.

"See, Adam wasn't even paying attention to us."

"Yes I was. I was just thinking about your decision and realised there was no way we'd make it out alive with any of your plans. Your plan doesn't have a chance of ending well, and mine does. A spirit within me has shown visions of the future many times before and they were always correct, and you've supposedly seen what it can do to those that make it angry."

Then as Adam was saying this, his teeth started to grow pointier as he grew taller.

"You have no idea what you're going to be getting yourself into when going with Seth's plan, but I can predict everything that will happen with mine, and I can say right now that if done right, my plan will end better than yours."

Then as Adam grew taller and more muscular, he yelled, "Now we don't have much time left because of this discussion, and if you don't follow us, I'll leave you all to follow your ridiculous plan, and die."

Everyone continued to stare in awe at Adam as he slowly returned to his 'normal' self and placed his hands on the ground. Then with much hesitation Josh, Harry and Seth walked upon them while Tom stuck with Ben and Bailey.

Everyone had become even more fearful of Adam than ever before, and Bailey asked Ben, "Why are we following Adam?"

Ben answered with, "I don't know, but those drains won't lead anywhere but death."

The World Above
New Frontier
Chapter 24
Driving to the Aquaport

Everyone had taken all the food they could carry and filled up their masks fully. Tom even did it in case they were separated from Ben, but Bailey didn't think it would be necessary since he'd always been safe within the shield.

As they had all made it to the sea carcumber safely with no fish seeing them, Adam tried to stretch his arms up to the door handle, but when they made it up there, he found out the door was locked. Then he decided that maybe they could all ride on top of the sea carcumber so he started to stretch Seth and Josh up. He decided that stretching everyone up by twos would be best since it was a long stretch.

Soon Josh and Seth managed to climb on top of the car and laid flat to not be seen, and because they couldn't stand up without falling over. Soon Bailey started to climb up Adams hand followed by Harry when he noticed the fish and yelled, "Hurry up, the fish are coming!"
Then as Adam heard that, he immediately tried to lift them up faster and made sure Harry and Bailey wouldn't fall.

Tom and Ben had noticed the fish as they told Adam to hurry up, just as he managed to stretch Bailey and Harry to the top, he allowed them to get pulled across to safety by Josh. Then Adam grabbed the top of the car and started to pull himself up, he instructed Ben and Tom to run under the sea carcumber.

It was too late for Ben and Tom to go up with him so they both ran under the car and looked up to see multitudes of pipes above them with some kind of fat sticking it all together. Then as Adam had pulled himself to the top of the car, he laid low with the others. The fish had walked to the doors on the sides of the car and were carrying groceries with them. The sea carcumber got unlocked and the fish hopped in. Then Ben signalled Tom to follow him as he stayed close by.

As the sea carcumber started to drive off, Ben and Tom reached up to the back of the sea carcumber and were lifting themselves up. Ben continued to lift his legs in the air as they were getting dragged across the ground. Tom managed to pull himself up and reached down to help pull up Ben. They sat balanced along the back of the sea carcumber, the others on the top thought they were either crushed or left behind.

Then as Seth and the others looked back at the drain and were prepared to jump back, Adam looked across at them as he said, "Don't bother jumping, this is the right decision, everything should be okay for all of us from now on."

As Josh, Bailey, Seth and Harry laid flat on the car, they hoped that Adam would be able to fight back against the spirit within so he could return. As they lay flat, they realised that the top was actually really slippery so they had to find a way into the sea carcumber for safety. Then they wondered if there was a boot in this weird version of a car.

"Hey Tom, lately you've been acting a little differently."

"How so?" asked Tom.

"Well, why have you been randomly saying things that I think are intended to be funny? For the situation we're in, it just doesn't seem relevant," asked Ben.

"Ben, have you seen how much stress has been created amongst all of us. We've seen people die. We've watched our whole world change. We can never find out if any of our friends and family are alive. All of us probably have some kind of Post-Traumatic Stress Disorder we're all hiding away. Then I found out that Rusheel had died, and that Regen, Nick and Jared became the enemy for some reason. All this death is actually starting to make me feel sick."

"Oh, right."

"I figured that any kind of humour, whether it was good or bad would help ease the situation we are in, and make our lives a little easier to live through. Baileys in on it as well since he seemed like he was suffering the worst and needed a little bit of positivity in his life.

I hope that you now understand the situation we're all in and why I'm doing this."

"Okay, I understand now."

"Oh and one other question. Do you think the fish are bad or villainy? I just wanted to hear your opinion on it since all I've seen the fish do is bad things."

"Well, you could look at it that way Ben. The fish are hunting us down and trying to capture us. They're also giving us no respect as beings and are prepared to treat us as pets. You could easily see them as the villains. Or you could see them as something else."

"What?" asked Ben.

"You could see them as acting human," muttered Tom.

Then as Ben thought about this for a moment, he realised that Toms perspective was surprisingly a reasonable one.

Tom realised what he said was weird so he added on with saying, "Anyway, this ledge we're sitting on doesn't seem very safe. I wonder if there's a way inside the boot?" Ben wasn't really thinking about that at the moment when Tom saw a handle. The others on the roof weren't really sure of this idea since it was really risky, and Ben kept telling Tom that Adam knew the fish were taking them exactly where they needed to go, but Tom didn't listen. Then as Adam and Seth slid along over to the back of the car, the boot opened up unexpectedly and nearly made them fall off.

Tom had reached the handle, pulled it, and made the door go flying upwards. Ben was thrown into the tow bar and hung on for his life. Then as Tom was still holding onto the boot, he started to slip. Then he fell... until he stretched his robot arm as far out as possible and grabbed the side of the car, pulling himself back. As the car slowed down, Ben managed to climb back onto the car and into the boot as it was parking.

Ben had already started to run inside as Tom stretched his way back. He followed behind Ben as he started to open one of the suitcases. Then as Tom heard doors opening, Ben fully opened the suitcase as they both jumped inside it. The fish wandered over to the boot and looked into it, wondering how it could have opened. But it was mainly glad that nothing had fallen out because the adult fish was skilled at packing for their interstate holiday. Then when he noticed the suitcase unzipped, he reached for it, tipped it vertically and zipped it up, thinking it smelled a little different than usual and figured it was nothing.

Then as the fish shut the boot, he wandered back to the driver's seat and started up the car.

When the boot was shut, everyone on the roof realised that the others may have lived and had the same plan, and as the seacarcumber was driving off, they all weren't sure what they were supposed to do next as the thirty-minute wait had begun.

The sea carcumber pulled into a parking spot as everyone on top of the seaicle laid flat to avoid being seen. The three fish hopped out of their car and everyone on top realised what had to be done. The bigger male fish opened up the boot and started to pull out the suitcases, not realising that part of one of the suitcases was drier than usual.

Bailey, Josh, Harry, Adam and Seth knew that they had to find a way into the suitcases within the boot when they realised someone had to be a distraction. Then as they sat there, not knowing what to do next, Adam knew exactly where they had to go. Someone would need to act as a sacrifice, although he didn't know who it should be. Then as the doors of the seaicle opened up and fish walked out of the car, Adam lost control of his body and was prepared to push Josh off the car since he was the closest to him, until Bailey lost balance and fell off it himself.

Immediately Adam regained his sense of control as Bailey slid off the car and landed on the older male fish.
The female one and the kid had unloaded their suitcases from the seaicle when suddenly a human had fallen onto the female one's husband.

As soon as Bailey fell, Seth realised this and reached over to him, but it was too late as Seth, Josh, Adam and Harry slid off the back of the car and landed on one of the suitcases.

Tom felt the others land near them as Ben was just awakening. Tom stretched up his arm and managed to slide the zipper along to open up the suitcase for the others to get in. The fish were still busy dealing with Bailey who had jumped on the male fish and started to slide down the back of his shirt. Bailey slid down the fish's shirt against the slimy scaly body until he reached an opening.

Tom opened up the suitcase as Josh was trying to get Seth to follow him inside as well. Ben crawled over to help them get inside. Then as Harry stood and tried to climb in by himself, Tom pulled him in instead. Then as Harry slipped up and fell into the suitcase, Adam followed from behind. Ben reactivated the shield around Josh and Seth and forced them both inside as well. Seth continued to struggle as he tried to get out and save Bailey, until he noticed him fall to the ground and have all of the fish watch him slip up and flop around on the pavement.

The kid was grossed out by the way Bailey was acting as he was dry and rough. Then as Bailey was struggling to breathe, he was just about to drown when spinning circles appeared around him. Then he shut his eyes and vanished into a blue blur, right when Seth got pulled back into the suitcase and missed Bailey's disappearance.

Tom was also concerned about where Bailey was since he helped Tom with staying positive. But now Bailey was gone.

And Tom started to lose all hope that things could get better since over time, things only ever got worse.

All of the fish were curious about what had happened and realised how impossible it was so they tried to walk it off, thinking that it never happened.
The female fish wandered over to the suitcase not realising part of it was drier than usual, and zipped up the zipper wondering how it even got open. The distraction that was caused by Bailey had bought everyone else enough time to hide without being seen. Then as the three fish got their suitcases and started to walk to the aquaport, the smaller fish whined, "My suitcase feels heavier than usual," and his dad replied, "Suck it up princess, shouldn't have packed so much stuff."

The fish rolled their suitcases behind them at the aquaport as the smaller fish was trying hard to get over the fact that its suitcase was heavy and had to put up with it. The fish got to the counter and placed their suitcases onto the conveyor belt and watched as they disappeared behind the plastic drapes. Everyone inside the suitcase felt really squashed as they dug into the disgustingly wet clothes and tried to rest as they didn't want to risk escaping and getting caught.

The fish boarded their plane as their suitcases got placed onto a loading truck with everyone somehow not getting detected by scanners. Then the loading truck drove to the plane as fish threw the suitcases into it. Everyone one in the suitcase got bounced around and rolled in the wet clothes as the suitcase landed in the plane and stopped moving when a whole bunch of other suitcases were thrown on top of them. The cargo door closed and all of the fish boarded the plane. When it closed, it started to drive across the runway and took off for a long flight.

The World Above
New Frontier
Chapter 25
Town of Ruin

Meanwhile, in the World Below, everyone wanted answers from Bailey.

"Look, for the last time, for very specific time travel reasons I can't say what happens to you lot in the future and why we've been teleporting to different places. I don't know anything about the war, and I don't know what is going to happen to us next. I only just realised that I wasn't even sent that far into the past, and that's it. Oh and Ben, like I've continuously said, I know you saw me drown in the World Above, but I vanished, appeared now and I don't know why." sighed Bailey

"Okay then, we understand you don't know anything, let's just get off that topic," said Michaela.

"So Ben, do you still know where we need to go to get to our destination?" asked Kate.

Ben reluctantly pulled out a map and looked around the area. He noticed that the plane was heading in the correct direction before it crashed so they just needed to walk.

"We need to go in the direction that the plane is facing," said Ben.

"That will take forever though, we need some kind of, car," said Bailey.

Then right away, spinning circles appeared and a car ended up near them.

"Wait, who bought that car here?" asked Bailey.

As no one could think of an answer, Kate and Michaela ran to the car to check to see if the keys were in there or not and they were. Tara called the guys over and as everyone jumped into their seats, Ben became the driver, started the car and headed in the direction of the plane wreckage.

As they drove closer to the wreckage, everyone looked away most of the time because of all the remains of bodies scattered everywhere. As Ben drove past most of the wreckage, he noticed that the plane was caught in some kind of plastic bag. He pulled over and wandered over to the giant plastic bag. Some of it was melting, but Ben was still able to examine it.

Looking over the remains of the plane, he realised that some humans also acted as an enemy at times. Humans acted as an enemy, about as often as fish acted well. He continued to think about this as the others were also curious about the plastic bag and all of the ones they landed on. Then as Kate got out of the car, she motioned everyone to get back in since what was coming to them was bigger than anything they had faced before.

Bailey was out of the car already as a bunch of Lego bricks came flying at him. Then Kate and Tara climbed back into the car and yelled for everyone to jump in and drive away. As they looked at what had appeared, everyone immediately jumped into the car as Ben drove away from the shipping container that was falling from above. Ben immediately floored it and drove away as the shadow of the container had passed them completely when Michaela yelled, "Don't drive away from it, drive to the side of it!"

Ben knew what she meant and turned the car to the left. The metal container was just about to land on them when Ben drove past the shadow, allowing for a narrow escape as the container fell.

"Ben, the way you were driving from it was the exact wrong way to drive from something like that. We could have died."

"I think that was the least of our problems Michaela," stuttered Ben.

Then as everyone looked at what was behind the shipping container, they noticed crushed cans of soft drink, cracked bottles, pieces of paper, multiple Lego bricks, take away containers, rubbish bags and other junk, all built up in a massive pile that looked to have been somehow getting even bigger, and was swarming all areas in that direction. The direction they needed to drive through.

The plane was completely wrecked. Even the hungry-ones had died. As Ben drove past the plane wreckage, he told everyone to hang on as he started to drive the car through the rubbish pile since there was no way around it. Glass started to scrape along the sides of the car and many different murky coloured mists went through it as well. The mists weren't toxic though. They kind of resembled regular soft drink smells. Cup containers flew past them and icy pole sticks bounced off the car, but then the plastic bags appeared. Ben tried to swerve around the plastic bags as they floated past and above them.

The rubbish didn't really seem that bad at first as Bailey looked outside and noticed lots of mini pieces of plastic drift past them and Tara noticed simple toys float past as well. Ben was swerving around as many things as he could when he noticed a soft drink called coral cola. He knew it resembled something, but couldn't work out what it was. There were all kinds of interesting things to see and they started to think it wasn't going to be as bad as they thought.

They drove around and noticed jagged pieces of glass sticking out of the ground as some rotting fish clothes drifted past. It didn't seem that bad, but the rubbish was taking over. It had covered all of the trees and the remaining houses in the area. There were dead animals that had choked on the rubbish everywhere, and people were rotting all over the road because of the plastic they swallowed by mistake. One person was rotting with a hook in his mouth. Someone else got strangled by a plastic bag.

As Ben drove through the rubbish infested area, he saw the remains of people who had been humaned and gutted by the fish. Then he saw some kind of animal choking on another plastic bag. Up ahead, Ben saw a humaning net right in front of them and tried to drive around it. Everyone looked around in amazement as Ben managed to swerve away from the net as a pole appeared behind it and hit the ground hard. The breeze was getting a little bit stronger and a piece of glass flew into the windscreen.

The glass was stuck halfway, but everyone was startled by it. Outside it was getting very hard to see as things continued to hit the car and damage it. Everyone was a little tense as no one knew what they could do to help.

Strange things were splattering all over the car and Ben couldn't just wipe them off with the wipers. Ben just drove through ignoring them, but as he got deeper into the rubbish pile, he noticed that more rubbish was appearing. After a while, it became difficult to even see where he was going at all. Then without a warning, he heard two wheels of the car pop as he had driven over some jagged glass.

Everyone else was tired and started to sleep since they had nothing they could do except to lock all of the doors. As Ben was falling asleep, he continued to hate the fish as they caused all of the rubbish and pollution that was destroying their environment and killing innocent lives.

All the fish ever did was kill humans. All the rubbish made him realise just how careless the fish were as well. He knew that everyone also believed that the fish were the true enemy in this. And that they all needed to be stopped. For the moment though, all they could hope was that the rubbish would all blow over eventually.

The World Above
New Frontier
Chapter 26
The Floating Dangers

"Ah. Everyone get up now!" yelled Bailey.
Michaela and Kate got up when they saw the hungry-one right
on their windscreen trying to break through. Ben also got up
and started up the car to drive away, but the other two tires
had been popped by the hungry-one so the car couldn't move.

Ben immediately tried to turn on his shield when he
remembered that he'd thrown it to Darian before. The hungry-
one started to smash its head against the windscreen. Blood
was trickling down its head and just as it was about to get
through, it smashed his head into the jagged piece of glass
sticking out and fell off the car.

Everyone knew that if that hungry-one got in, they'd all be
dead and that just made them all want to get away from there.
The hungry-one on the ground was shaking all over as blood
was trickling all over his head. Everyone had gotten out of the
car and had experienced the strong breeze as a newspaper
appeared and blew onto the car.

Tara was just waking up as Bailey and Ben left the car. Tara
climbed out too to see what attacked them, and when she saw
the hungry-one, she pulled out her knife to finish it off until
she remembered how innocent the women looked after killing
her on the plane by accident.

This caused Tara to drop her knife and fall to the ground as she tried to get over what she had done. Then as the hungry-one eventually bled to death, Tara regained her thought patterns as she got up and continued going on with the others. Kate and Michaela wandered out as the giant newspaper ripped in half with most of it getting blown away. Then Kate noticed Tara's knife on the ground, picked it up, and kept it with her in case it was needed. There was broken glass everywhere with all kinds of rubbish as well. They pushed through the rubbish as it was thickening around them.

Bailey was pushing something away when he cut his finger on an opened can. Then nails and pieces of metal flew past them. Many different kinds of fluids and gasses went through them tasting mouldy and disgusting. Then as more rubbish bags were opening around them, they were starting to suffocating in the rubbish. Kate poked her whole hand into one of the rubbish bags and had something slimy run down it.

Michaela continued to look out for glass when a piece of paper came floating towards her. Tara was trying to pull Kate out of the rubbish when a dead crab fell on her.
Then as Ben was trudging through the mess, he saw a dead person floating towards him with a plastic ring around his neck. Ben stood back and stepped on some glass making him fall over in pain. Bailey was stepping back from all this when the newspaper on the car blew off, making him realise they'd gone nowhere. Then as everyone got out of their little situations, they noticed a cold breeze around them and saw all of the rubbish floating in a certain direction, away from where they wanted to go.

As they tried to fight the breeze, they slowly split up from each other as each of them were pushing away as much rubbish as they could. Then as they were all pushing through the rubbish, they felt the ground shake underneath them and they all knew what this shake was. They were heading towards another trench. Tara trudged along the best she could when she watched Kate fall over. Then as Kate nearly fell into a spreading hole, Tara knew how she could redeem herself from killing an innocent person.

That was when Tara grabbed Kate's wrist, and used all her strength to pull her out. This caused Tara to slip up and fall into the trench, only to end up vanishing into a blue light. Then as Kate realised what Tara had done, she tried to push through the rubbish to see if she was okay, but Ben grabbed her arm and pulled her away from the cracks formed by the trench. As rubbish surrounded all of them, Michaela was able to find Bailey and scrambled over to him.

They all felt the rumble of the trench slowly spreading towards them and soon everyone just gave up trying to fight the breeze and stopped doing anything. Bailey crawled over to Ben and Kate as they both fell over. Then Michaela crawled over to them as she fell. They huddled close together since there was nothing they could do. The cracks had spread past them, and they waited for the trench to consume them.

They slowly slid down and were struggling to see anything when Bailey looked up and noticed a net pushing the rubbish away from them. Then before the four of them fell, the net caught them and they started to get pulled through the rubbish and on to the surface. They were pulled into The World Above where they could see the amount of rubbish in the entire area. There was rubbish all around them for kilometres, and it didn't even seem to end there.

"Nice work Emma, you were finally able to save some humans like you said you would," said Emma's friend.

"Yeah I know right, good thing I convinced you to come with me," Emma said.

"Whatever, just clean them up so we can release them."

"Sure okay."

The fish emptied them into a container and looked very disappointed to see how they were.

"It's such a shame air life's environment has become like this. Poor humans. I wonder if they can even imagine a world with no rubbish?" asked Emma.

Kate and Michaela stood up, trying to search the area for a way out when one of the fish picked up Bailey and pulled him out. There was nothing the others could do as they were still catching their breaths. Bailey looked around and was struggling to breathe and thought his head was coming off. He soon realised that the fish were cleaning him up after saving his life.

When the fish was done cleaning the rubbish off Bailey, it put him into an even cleaner container. Then as it did the same thing with everyone else, they started to wonder what the fish wanted to do with them.

"Come on, let's go see if we can save more humans," said Emma.

Then as the fish drove their boat along the rubbish-filled ocean, they stopped another time to rescue some other people. When the other people were cleaned up, they were thrown into the same container as the others and seemed just as worried as they were.

The boat continued to drive on in the direction Ben wanted to go, but he was starting to run out of time. As they tried to relax in the container, Michaela and Kate moved over to the others to see who they were. When Kate asked who they were, one of them stammered, "My name is Seth, and these are my mates Rusheel, Regen and Jared."

Ben and Bailey then both looked at each other as Bailey said, "Well this just got really confusing."

The World Above
New Frontier
Chapter 27
Wanted

In the World Above...
The plane landed after a couple of hours had passed. Everyone woke up as fish started to stack up suitcases onto another loading truck again. The suitcase everyone was in got picked up and was thrown into the loading truck as more suitcases landed on top of them. No one inside the suitcase said anything as they wanted to make as little noise as possible. After unloading the suitcases onto the conveyor belt, they ended up exiting the plastic drapes where the fish grabbed the suitcases, rolled them out to a rented car and drove to a hotel. No one was sure what had actually happened to them or where they were now, except for the spirit within Adam.

As everyone stayed still inside the suitcase, Adam started to sense another image appearing in his head. He tried to study and examine the image as much as he could and only identified the name of some air-food restaurant. Then Adam knew where they had to go next. The fish threw their suitcases onto the floor of their apartment and as the parents started to unpack their suitcases, the kid decided to do that later as he just wanted to sit in bed and play on his game. His suitcase was slid under the bed and that's when everyone decided to start their escape.

The two older fish turned on something that looked like a television and it showed a fish sitting in a news desk. The television was turned up a little louder and as everyone climbed out of the suitcase, they looked at the television and heard the reporter talking. It was difficult to understand what the fish was saying, but they all got the gist of what was going on and made them realise that all the fish were on the lookout for walking humans.

On the news, it said that there had been sighting all over the state of walking humans and that there was a bounty on them. All sea creatures above thought it was impossible for a human to walk around in their world and breathe, thinking that the news was tricking them. Then video footage appeared from security cameras in a Corals store and a Human and Chips shop.

This was followed by photographic evidence from a Corals worker that showed two humans standing in a milk container. Then a witness who worked at a supermarket appeared on the TV and said, "Yeah, I've seen the walking humans and they're able to breathe, walk and climb things in our world. Actually, they can do more, I-I witness two of them teleport to another part of the store. I tried to get them an- and they kind of just vanished and reappeared somewhere else."

Then the news showed an interview with another fish as he stated, "Yeah I've seen the humans walk around. They are way more dangerous than they appear. One human had a robot arm and knocked me out with it. Another human had some sort of guns in use. But that's not the freakiest part. I've seen the humans come back from the dead. They can never be injured. One merged with me and became a split personality. The humans are dangerous. Stay away from them at all costs."

Then when that interview ended, the news reporter said, "Mhmm very interesting, actually I know someone who claimed that a dead human attacked him. It seemed to possess his body parts and cause him to do things he would never have done before. Sounds like a human invasion may be starting right."

"Yeah, that would be a weird type of war we'd have with them," said the co-news reporter.

"Now for other news, many injured at a beach after missiles were fired at people by… other humans. Okay, maybe let's move on from this weird human invasion topic we seem to be focused on okay."

Afterwards, the news report said that no one was allowed to harm the walking humans, but would get a reward if they were found and brought to the police. The police would take them to scientists to study them and work out why they were able to walk. There was also mention of time getting frozen, but there wasn't much proof on that topic.

Ben and the others weren't sure what to think of this news report, but knew that they were now wanted by curious sea creatures that wanted to experiment on them.

Ben kept the shield running with Harry and Tom so that they could walk while Adam continued to carry Josh and Seth. After lots of failed attempts, Harry gave up on the idea of walking in the World Above since it just seemed impossible for him. He realised he'd been turned into a freak for no reason. The fish hadn't noticed them moving about as they slid through the door to leave. Long after they were gone, the male fish called his son down to unpack his suitcase, and when the kid climbed down and opened it, he realised everything was drier than before and that it had the bad stench of human.

Ben and the others went down the corridor as slowly and quietly as possible with no fish walking past and reached some stairs. It took a while, but they eventually got down. Ben checked his watch wondering why there weren't any fish about and saw that it was around two o'clock in the afternoon. Then as they all got to the bottom of the staircase, two fish appeared in front of them and stared with their mouths open. Then they slowly pulled out their phones and started recording the humans.

"Corey, are you seeing what I'm seeing?"

"If what you're seeing is walking humans, then yes A.J., I am seeing what you're seeing,"

The humans decided to just walk past the two fish as they were just recording them and started to follow from behind.

"Can you believe it, those humans are walking and breathing right in front of us," stammered Corey.

"Yeah I know right, it's just crazy, should we capture them mate?"

"Na, let's just let them do their thing,"

Then the fish walked off leaving everyone thinking they dodged a bullet.

They got out of the hotel and walked down one of the streets as unnoticeably as they could. Sometimes little fish would find them, but the streets were covered in so many fish, the little ones that saw them would be soon pulled away. Even though they weren't being noticed by anyone, they found it difficult to find the restaurant that Adam saw in his vision. As they all searched around, Adam continually heard a voice in his head tell him what direction to go and everyone would follow him as they had nowhere else to go to.

As they continued along the path trying not to get stepped on, occasionally fish would see them and take a photo of them, but just move on. The fish didn't want to bother the humans because they were interested in how they could walk and breathe, but they didn't want to be the cause of something bad happening to them. Since that news report came out, they actually became safer from the fish than before. The voice in Adams' head continued to give him directions, but it was getting more and more difficult as they couldn't see any of the shops around them.

Then as they walked onto a different part of the path, less and less fish were around them and eventually just the occasional one. As they continued walking, one of the fish put its foot in front of them and stopped them from walking. At first, everyone felt provoked, until a bunch of seaicles started driving in front of them. As everyone was waiting behind the foot, Adam looked over it and saw the place they needed to go to.
"Hey Tamara, I just stopped the humans that are walking from going in front of a seaicle. I think I saved their lives."
Then as the road became free, Tamara said, "Good job Kira, now let's go and let them do their thing, come on."
The two fish walked off feeling good as Adam signalled everyone to follow him across the road and was able to see the area much clearer since they were in front of all the fish. After looking around for a bit, they noticed the store they needed to go that was across the street.

After everyone got across the road, they all started to head into the store when they all realised that the place they were entering was a restaurant that was really busy. As they wandered into the store not knowing where to go, one of the fish that was dining at the restaurant saw them, but instead of trying to catch them himself. He decided to call the cops on them.

"Down the drain, go down it!" the voice said. Then it disappeared. Making Adam realise what they needed to do. All of the fish in the restaurant tried to ignore the humans, as they didn't want to be involved in any police work. All they did was stare and take pictures of them.

As they were nearing a bathroom door, Seth heard sirens behind them and realised they all needed to hurry. Seth told everybody and as they got closer to the door, they realised there was a handle they had to pull. Then cop cars appeared at the front of the store.

"Hey Dad, can Zoe and I open up the door so the humans can get past?" asked one of the fish.

"No Caitlin, you and Zoe don't want to be part of police business," answered her dad.

"Please, they're not going to make it if we don't help out though."

Adam was prepared to stretch his arms up, but the police had come through the door and were about to get them when Caitlin got her sister Zoe, ran out in front of them and opened the door. The humans ran through the door and through the left corridor, as they were closest to it. Caitlin ran through the door as well and opened the second door for the humans to get past. Zoe stayed behind to block off the police fish.

The police pushed past Zoe as her dad got her and pulled her away. Then as the police ran through, they tried to push past Caitlin yelling "Stop, stop, you don't know what you're doing!" and pushed past her when she had an idea.
"Help, help, these bad men are hurting me! Please, I need help!" and that's when all the police backed away from her a little, allowing her to run onwards towards the humans.

The police barged through the toilet door as Adam stretched his arms up and got Seth and Tom on the toilet allowing them to jump in. When Seth jumped in, Tom stayed behind. He turned his robot arm into a missile launcher and aimed it at the police fish. They were intrigued with this weapon, wondering what it was made of. Then Caitlin managed to push through the fish and ended up running to the toilet behind Tom. She was a young fish and wasn't bothered by Tom's weaponry. When she looked down and saw the human trying to run through the pipes of the toilet. She pushed the flusher.

Adam started to lower his hands and let Ben, Josh and Harry walk onto them to get lifted up. The police fish continued closer towards them very cautiously. Then Tom lost patience with them and was about to fire, until he realised it might scare the female fish helping them escape. The police continued to move forward and as they were able to reach them, Ben, Josh and Harry had started to climb up the toilet. Then as the three of them prepared to jump in it, the fish reached forward and grabbed Harry.

The fish was wearing gloves and had a strong grip as it grabbed Harry and pulled him away before he managed to climb up. Ben and Josh realised this but was unable to help as they wouldn't be able to do much. As Harry was getting pulled away, he looked back to show how different he looked as the fish dropped him onto the floor. Adam let Josh jump into the toilet when Harry turned back and wondered if he was even needed with them as he'd always felt like an outcast tagging along with them for no reason.

Stressing out over seeing Harry get captured, Ben turned to Tom and asked him,
"Hey bro, do you have anything thing funny to say about the situation we're in right now? You know, to create more positivity for me."
Tom did think of jokes to say about the toilet they stood upon and prepared to jump into, but he knew that they'd all be crap. It didn't matter though. It seemed almost impossible to show off any positivity at the moment.
"You know Ben, after seeing Bailey die, I don't believe that positivity can be created anymore. So no. I have nothing to say about the situation we're in. All hope is lost."
Then Tom pushed Ben into the toilet as Tom was done talking to him. Tom's main mission was to survive and defend others. That's simply all he had left.

Harry was too far from anyone to be helped out, and he knew it was now his time to act independently. He thought back to all the times he practiced walking in the past, and stood up straight by himself. He was trying to stay balanced as the police fish stalled a little by watching Harry stand straight and walk forward.

Then as Harry realised he could walk around by himself, he saw Adam look at him as Adam wondered why Harry wasn't walking towards him. Harry knew what he wanted to do. He still wanted to explore The World Above since he knew that he could never be accepted in the World Below anymore because of how he looked.

Then as Harry turned his back to Adam, the fish picked him up. Harry couldn't think of any way of escaping the fish's grip when the fish grabbed out a plastic container and dropped him into it, leaving him trapped. Ben and Josh had already been pushed into the toilet by Tom, and Caitlin pulled down the flusher to let both of them go down.

Adam was still pulling himself up when the police fish realised they stalled a little by watching Harry stand before. Then the fish went to reach down for him, but Caitlin immediately scooped him up and tossed him into the bowl, then pushed the flush button as the police yelled out for her to stop. Then right as the fish reached for Tom, he turned his robot arm into a missile launcher once again.

The fish saw this and restrained from grabbing Tom since a missile was seen sliding into the missile launcher. Caitlin stood away from Tom as he held his weapon high in front of him, right as he said, "This is for everyone that had died in the New Frontier, and now we'll fight back!"

Immediately, Tom fired a missile into the ceiling, causing the fish to duck for cover as it fell on top of them in pieces.

Tom shot the ceiling above the police fish so Caitlin wasn't harmed. Then he pulled down on the flusher and jumped into toilet to get sent into the pipes with the others. Caitlin's dad ran through the remains of the ceiling, got her out of there and left the restaurant. Parts of the ceiling had fallen onto the police fish and had bruised them, leaving cuts all over themselves. They were disappointed that not all the humans were caught, but they had one. They had Harry, and he looked like something that could give away a lot of information about what was really going on, even if he looked like an abomination to nature.

The World Above
New Frontier
Chapter 28
Flushed Away

Everyone thought it was kind of gross sliding down the pipes of a fish's toilet, but it was a way out that they had to use to get to the World Below. Some of them were finding it more difficult to slide down the pipes properly, but they managed to get through. They all liked the fact that they were surrounded by air again, but they were so squashed against the pipes that they were still struggling to breathe, then a thought occurred to Josh. Waste from toilets don't head toward the ocean, they go to DE filtering places where water gets purified, and junk gets thrown into the disposal.

The police fish didn't want to just stop going after the escaping humans and they had gained a plan. One of them went over and grabbed a toilet plunger and started pushing it down the toilet. The humans in the pipes started to feel something pulling them back. Everyone was struggling to crawl through the pipes and the air pulling them back wasn't helping. They all pushed further trying to get through and ignoring the stuff around them. Then air started flowing forward for them as Seth managed to pull himself out of the pipe with Josh following from behind and landing in the sewer.

The police were trying even harder pushing up and down faster on the plunger as Ben, Adam and Tom were struggling to get through. Tom had his robot arm out in front of him so he was able to pull himself along with it. As Adam squeezed through, he stretched out his arms to help push Ben out.

While the fish police were using the plunger, some of the other fish police headed out the restaurant to start searching the sewers. The fish were desperately wanting the humans that got away and were willing to do anything to get them. The police fish that had Harry made sure the lid was sealed tight so that there was no way for Harry to escape. He just sat there not knowing what to do next.

Ben was slipping inside the pipe as he was getting pulled out and Adam gave him a good shove which pushed him further. Ben grabbed the edges of the pipe and pulled himself out with Adam following from behind. Then Tom stretched out his robot arm and accidentally punctured a hole in the pipe to finally get pulled out and land in the sewer with everyone else.

Josh and Seth had already started to go and explore the right side of the sewer to see where it was going when they started to hear noises of splashing footsteps up ahead with the noises of fish talking. Neither of them knew how the police fish got down there so quickly but were prepared to escape.

Then as the fish were getting closer to them, Seth and Josh allowed themselves to go under air again and felt more sprinting power in their legs. Then as the two of them hid under air, the fish started to walk past them, wondering where the humans went as they continued to search for them.

Seth and Josh ran past the fish quickly, but noticeably as the fish followed from behind. Ben, Tom and Adam were wondering where Josh and Seth had gone when they saw them run past quickly with the sounds of police fish behind them. Adam, Ben and Tom noticed that they had more sprinting power in their legs as well so immediately they sprinted through the sewer faster than usual as the fish soon became long gone.

None of them were really tired from the run, but they soon had to stop as there was a massive hole in front of them. Then it dawned on all of them that not all pipes lead out to the ocean and especially not toilet pipes. They all figured that they'd be able to swim past the fish, but there was a lot of them. They also didn't have anywhere else to go.

Everyone was backed up against the edge of the hole as the fish were reaching for them. And that was when Ben pushed everyone off the edge and made them all fall into the hole. The fish weren't sure what they needed to do to get the humans back but in frustration, they turned away since the humans were gone. Ben and the others that were falling noticed the fish walk back, causing them to believe that they had escaped. Then a flashing red light appeared in front of them. They landed at the bottom of the pit and started to get pulled towards a dark tunnel where they would be discarded and destroyed.

They all tried to fight the wind drawing them in, but it was too strong. That was when a flying drone appeared above them with a net. The drone frantically swished the net back and forth trying to get the humans, but it missed every time. The police fish were desperately trying to get the drone to catch the humans and record footage of them. Everyone was getting pulled downstream as the air was going to pull them into some kind of strainer.

They were pushed against the strainer unable to move as the drone continued towards them. Then blue spinning circles spun around them all. The drone continued to edge closer with the camera recording everything in sight as the spinning circles spun faster and faster creating a blue light that surrounded everyone. Then as the drone came closer, it swung its net at them and the blue light surrounded that. Then immediately, everyone, including the drone vanished.

The fish were confused by what they were seeing next as it was just glowing spirals everywhere as the drone reappeared smashing into the side of a pipe. Everyone reappeared stumbling out of the pipe and fell slowly to the ground. When everyone had landed, Seth and Josh looked up and noticed the drone appear out of the pipe as well, making everyone run away to dodge the incoming drone. No one was harmed when the drone crashed, but it wasn't moving anymore as the propellers were smashed.

The middle part of it still seemed intact and the glowing red light was still on. No one was even sure how they got out of the pit. How they teleported somewhere. The drone continued to look at them so Tom grabbed the front of it with his robot arm and crushed it, so it couldn't record more of what they did.

The fish looking at their monitor was speechless. Not only had their drone teleported somewhere, but one of the humans had crushed it with a robot arm. Then they looked back at the human they had caught realising just how powerful air life may have become. Harry didn't want to help give out information to the fish. He didn't even know how to, as he couldn't speak to them. But somehow they'd find a way. Even if it meant pulling him apart, bit by bit.

The World Above
New Frontier
Chapter 29
Frozen Air

After Tom drove away from the Time-Correction-Squares in
the World Below...
He had been driving Darian, Kelly and Hayley for a few hours
as they rested most of the way. There was a specific place
they needed to get to and nothing really life threatening
happened to them throughout the whole drive. They were
going along a freeway most of the time, and it was starting to
get cold. Darian started to wake up, wondering how long she
had slept for when Tom answered and they just sat there
quietly with small talk.

Soon Kelly woke up, looked out the window and saw ice form
on it. She knew it was cold, but she didn't think it was cold
enough for ice to freeze over.
"Hey Tom, can you turn up the heater, it's getting kind of
cold," asked Kelly.
"Okay, it was fine a while ago, but now it has suddenly gotten
really cold."
As Tom turned on the heater, Hayley also started to get up.
Ice was forming across the windscreen and it was making it
harder for Tom to see through it.

Then as Tom continued to drive on trying hard to see through
the ice, he started to get drowsy and started to shut his eyes.
He had done this kind of driving before, but he hadn't had a
proper rest in ages. Then his vision started to get a little blurry

as the car wobbled a little, and that's when his head dropped onto the steering wheel making him fall sideways and turn the car off the road. Then as Darian noticed Tom fall, she immediately pulled him back up, making him wake up and turn the wheel back, but the car slid on the icy road uncontrollably, causing it to flip onto its side and leaving everyone stunned.

The frost continued to cover the car as Tom was wondering what went wrong since the car was never turned enough to cause this. There were no serious injuries and everyone tried to climb out of the car a little shaken, but being able to walk. Tom was awake now, but still drowsy. They were all extremely lucky that no one was seriously injured and instead were just cold and sore.

They couldn't do very much at the time so they walked over to the nearby town to stay in a warm store for a bit. They went over to the closest store and tried to open it, but even with Tom's robot arm, he couldn't budge the door as it became completely frozen over. He could have opened it eventually, but if the door was frozen, the inside wouldn't be any warmer.

Darian and Kelly walked to the store next to it but when they tried to turn the handle, they immediately let go as it was ice shut as well. Darian and Kelly wandered back over to Hayley and Tom realising the entire door was completely frozen over. Then Hayley threw a rock at the store window and smashed it. It was much colder inside, but Hayley and Kelly were still willing to see what was inside while Darian stayed back with Tom as he felt drowsy from driving for so long.

As Kelly and Hayley walked further into the freezing store, they started to feel a warm breeze ahead of them. They continued along and saw a door behind the counter. They slowly opened it to find some people trying to keep warm by a fire. The three they hadn't met before immediately turned around looking a little confused. Then they looked over at Kelly and Hayley, and turned back to face the fire.

"Um so what happened here guys?" asked Hayley.

"It got cold, so everyone left to get warm.
But we wanted to stay. The cold will go soon.
We have enough food to live."

Then the three of them stayed quiet and Hayley and Kelly decided that maybe they needed to get away from there. They went over to the broken window to see Darian heading back to the car with Tom. Kelly and Hayley followed as they wondered what they were actually going to do with the overturned car. They all made it back safely and tried to hug each other for warmth.

As Kelly and Hayley tried to get warm, they looked above and noticed a layer of frozen air above them that had seemingly just formed since it was dripping small smoke bombs everywhere. The frozen air looked like dark rain clouds covering the surface of their world, but there seemed to be pieces of water from the World Above frozen within the dark clouds somehow. Then further across the frozen air, they looked through the dark clouds and saw two teenaged looking fish throwing stones in order to break it for fun.

They figured that in this new world, it was seemingly snowing in the World Above and was freezing everything in the World Below.

Tom noticed frost appearing on them when Darian slipped on the ice. Then Tom grabbed the side of the car and lifted it right side up again. He pushed it on the road and was exhausted, falling over from the cold as frost formed over his head. Kelly and Hayley crawled over to the car as Tom realised why they even crashed. The road was completely frozen over and they had walked so slowly over it that no one noticed. Tom knew the door handles would be as cold as the shop doors so he stretched his robot arm to open the two closest doors.

The car seemed to be still running even after the crash so it was getting warmer the whole time. Kelly and Hayley both tried to help each other get inside the car to feel the hot breeze and warm them up. Then Darian and Tom helped each other to stumble over to the car as well. Kelly and Hayley were hugging each other for more warmth and realised Tom wasn't able to drive safely anymore.

He was exhausted so Hayley crawled to the front seat while Kelly shut the door and moved over. Darian had frost all over her and Tom was beginning to collapse from the cold as well. Then with one final push Tom stretched his robot arm into the car and pulled himself inside, but Darian collapsed outside the car.

Tom decided to stretch out his bionic arm and pulled Darian inside as well. Then immediately shut the door. He was glad he turned on the heater before the crash and that was when he decided to rest. As they all rested, the frost continued over the car and over all of the windows. Then as Hayley turned the key to make sure the car was still drivable, the engine started and they were able to drive, but Hayley didn't actually know where Tom wanted to go while Darian and Kelly sat in the back seat watched all the frost form.

The three people inside the store continued to sit by the fire not really knowing what they were actually going to do when the cold went away. They were really only quiet and rude because they hadn't talked to anyone in days and simply felt alone and isolated. Then as they looked at the fire, they noticed that the top part of the flame was turning green.

They didn't really think much about it until they noticed the glowing green thing was spreading across the entire flame and lines were appearing forming glowing squares. Then the glowing squares spread further than the fire and that's when the fire completely stopped moving and turned cubic.

The three of them immediately shuffled backwards as the glowing green squares spread across the fireplace and onto the walls. Then they stood up slowly wondering what the green squares were so one of them bent over to it. Then as the other two were stepping back, their brother reached down and touched the glowing green squares and stood back up again looking at his fingers and noticed the green squares spreading across it. Then it spread across his hand, and then he couldn't move it anymore and realised he was in trouble.

The green squares continued to spread up the guy's arm, but he wasn't sure what to do to stop it. They all immediately ran out of their store, not caring about their broken window and ran for the others at the car. The green squares spread across the entire floor and along the shop counter. The ground was really slippery so they had to be careful where they stood. Then they saw a car start up not far from them. The guy that touched the green squares looked at his hand again and realised it was spreading across his entire body and down his legs.

Ice was forming on the windscreen but Hayley was able to see the others running towards them, but also noticed the green squares spreading across the face of one of the guys. Then as the green squares spread across his entire body, one of the others reached out to him and grabbed his arm.
"Come on, you can still make it."
"No, I don't think I can."
And that's when he turned completely blocky and disappeared into the glowing green squares. Then as the two of them looked up, they saw Time-Correction-Squares appear on the frozen air above them, dripping small smoke bombs of Time-Correction-Squares everywhere.

They both jumped into the car begging to go with them and Hayley just figured they had to go straight so that's what she did. She managed to dodge the Time-Correction-Squares on the tiny smoke bombs as she tried to swerve the car around them, but the glowing squares in their store continued to spread all over and onto other stores. Hayley started to drive faster, trying to make sure the car didn't slip again. Then as Tom tried to wake up, he saw where they were and looking at his map, told Hayley to go left so that's what she did. They had escaped the glowing squares again and Hayley ended up on a straight road that was icy, but still okay to drive on.

What they didn't realise was that the Time-Correction-Squares spread over most of the frozen layer of air above them, and constantly had smoke bombs covered in the Time-Correction-Squares dripping all over the top of the car. Then-

Time Correction-Squares spread over the back wheel of the car, over the boot and through the roof.

The girl that grabbed the guys hand looked at her hand and jumped in fright as hers was covered in the Time-Correction-Squares and was spreading across her entire body. Freaking out, Darian and Kelly tried to sit away from her as she accidentally touched her brother leaning over from the boot. Then the Time-Correction-Squares spread across the front chairs and continued across Hayley's back.

Tom had already opened up the door and immediately jumped out. He rolled against the icy road which left burns and deep cuts covering his whole body. Tom continued to try and get away from the car as the squares completely spread all over it and everyone inside. Then as Tom stumbled away as fast as he could, he saw the tiny smoke bombs covered in the Time-Correction-Squares land everywhere.

He also noticed the glowing squares spreading over everything around him and up his body since tiny smoke bombs landed on him. He knew he couldn't escape, and the longer he stayed away from them, the further he'd be sent back. So as he turned around, he saw the car turn blocky, have everyone fall apart and all disappear into the ground.
The teenaged fish above were still throwing rocks at the frozen air for fun, when one of the fish threw a rock so hard, it smashed through the frozen layer of air covered in Time-Correction-Squares.
The Time-Correction-Squares spread across Tom, causing him to turn blocky. Then looking above, he noticed giant blocks of air covered in the Time-Correction-Squares falling right above him. Then when a giant piece of frozen air

smashed his blocky remains into the ground, he was gone and **time reset.**

The World Above
New Frontier
Chapter 29
Frozen Air

They both jumped into the car begging to go with them and Darian just figured they had to go straight so that's what she did. She managed to dodge the frost on the bumpy rocks as she tried to swerve the car around them, but the frost in their store continued to spread all over and onto other stores. Darian started to drive faster, trying to make sure the car didn't slip again. Then as Tom tried to wake up, he saw where they were and looking at his map, told Darian to go left so that's what she did. They had escaped the frost in that certain area and Darian ended up on a straight road that was icy, but still okay to drive on.

What they didn't realise was that the frost spread over most of the frozen layer of air above them, and constantly had smoke bombs covered in nothing dripping all over the top of the car. Then the frost spread over the back wheel of the car, over the boot and through the roof.

The girl that grabbed the guys hand looked at her hand and jumped in confusion as hers was covered in the frost and wasn't spreading across her entire body. Confused, the other guy tried to sit away from her as she accidentally touched him leaning away from the seat. Then the frost didn't spread across the front chairs and didn't continue across Darian's back.

Then as Tom already closed the door and hadn't planned on jumping out, he noticed tiny smoke bombs dripping everywhere. Then looking further ahead, saw the seemingly teenaged fish throw a big stone towards the frozen air, causing it to smash above them. Darian noticed this and started to swerve around the frozen layers of air falling around them. Then when they passed all the falling pieces, a giant piece of frozen air above them snapped off the rest of it and fell towards them. Darian immediately pushed down the accelerator and drove beneath it.

The giant piece of frozen air landed and just missed them as it smashed through the tow bar and shattered into air particles across the road. Then as frost formed over everything around them and everyone was coming to terms with what had just happened, Darian asked, "Hey, my name is Darian and his name is Tom, what are your names… and why did you decide to come with us?"
"Oh, um, my name is Amanda, and this is my brother, Shane," answered Amanda.
"We left because we realised it was becoming so cold that we wouldn't last long and thought it would be a better idea to go with you guys since we haven't talked to other people in ages," said Shane.

"Mhmm, is anyone here feeling a little bit of Déjà vu? I swear this seems kind of familiar," asked Tom.
"Nope, everything seems fine, and I'm pretty sure you're just imagining things," replied Darian.
"I know, I bet I am just imagining things, but I feel like other people were meant to be here," stammered Tom.
"Who, do you have a name for them?" asked Darian.

"No, but I'm pretty sure someone came here with Amanda and Shane. Was there ever another person with you guys?" asked Tom.

"Well yeah, I guess, but he left months ago before the frost started because there were predictions it would freeze over," said Shane.

"Yeah, but I'm sure that there may have been other people with us even before we got here."

"Na, I don't think so. I mean before we got here, it was only you and me in the car Tom," said Darian.

"Are you sure there weren't others with you Darian before we got here. Any close friends?" asked Tom.

"Well yes, I knew someone named Kelly, but after weeks of trying to survive in this new world, we got separated and I was left with my other friend Amilia. It was only the two of us so it was easy to stay with each other and didn't give us any reason to move around much in the human trawling boat."

Darian continued, "It was horrible. On one of the conveyor belts, I saw a woman up ahead gasping for breath, but I was too far away to help out. I always think I imagined her being there though since she seemed to have vanished within a blue blur. Anyway, something made Amilia and I separate away from each other and we were placed into separate slots leading into a machine. Luckily time froze and allowed me to escape, but it was too late for Amilia as she ended up further in front of me. I would go on, but I was by myself until Tom came."

No one knew what to say after that as Amanda and Shane sat there trying to work out what had happened to Darian to cause all that.

Tom wasn't sure what to do with this information because he was still confused by the Déjà vu, even though it couldn't have happened before. It would mean that something had to have changed history. Then he remembered the Time-Correction-Squares, wondering if they had a part in this. He wasn't sure so he decided to piece together what had happened to him so far. So he spent the next few minutes thinking back around three weeks ago, back when all of this first began.

The World Above
New Frontier
Chapter 30
Human Aid

After being saved from the rubbish...
Ben and Bailey were very confused when looking at Rusheel, Regen and Jared, wondering how they got there since they were meant to be dead. Seth went over to Kate and Michaela as he wanted to introduce himself better while the others talked.

"Hey Ben," whispered Rusheel.
"This is very important so listen to me okay. You can't be seen by Seth at all because his future-self said he'd never seen anyone like you in the past. Oh yeah, by the way, that's not the Seth you know. That's past Seth."
Since Bailey was listening in on the conversation, he sighed, "Oh great, now I'm getting a headache."

"Wait a minute Jared and Regen. You two became the hungry-ones right, and you Rusheel, I heard you shrivelled into dust. How are you guys still alive and here right now?"
"We don't know. Just before I was about to die, spinning circles appeared around me and I blacked out," said Rusheel.
"Same with us, although we're fine now. We saw colourful spirals around both of us and ended up here being completely fine," said Jared.

"All of us ended up in the same area and saw Seth, thinking it was him and realised it was his past self. We still decided to tag along with him anyway though."

"For important time travel reasons, try not to be seen by Seth's past self Ben. Bailey, I think it's important if you end up staying with us after this."

Then as tiny spinning circles appeared around his head, Bailey said, "Okay then."

"So Ben, what are you doing here anyway?"

"I got sent back in time to bring Kate and Michaela with me to... a, safe place, but why do you guys have to go. Why not just come with us?" asked Ben.

"Seth's past self can't know who you are, but I think he has to know who we are. It's all complicated and hard to explain, but this has to happen."

"Okay then."

Then as Seth was done introducing himself, he started to walk back to the others. Ben decided to hide behind them when he got an idea. Ben stretched his jumper over his head to try and hide his face, and when Seth looked at him, he just saw Ben as some weird guy sitting alone in a corner. The others liked his plan, but when Kate saw him, she went to see if he was okay.

Ben said he was fine and just told her he was thinking about stuff so she went back over to the others. Ben was thinking about how these fish decided to save them for some reason. This made him question whether or not all fish were bad, but he didn't care about that anymore so he waited to be released.

The fish had driven the boat out of the massive rubbish pit, and when they thought it was safe for the humans to be free,

Emma picked up the bucket, swished it around a little to get the hidden junk off, and tipped them all back into the ocean, hoping that they wouldn't head back into the trash and that they'd stay safe.

Everyone in the box fell over and tripped up as more junk appeared in the air that had come off them. Then as they were tipped out of the boat and back into their world, they all thought they were going to splatter, but instead of falling fast, they fell slowly and landed safely. Ben figured they'd be safe from the fall as the gravity was slowly changing, but the others were still confused at what happened and decided that anything could really happen in this new world.

Rusheel, Jared and Regen then signalled Bailey to go with them, and waved goodbye to Ben, Kate and Michaela. Kate and Michaela weren't really sure why they had to split up and were about to follow the others until Ben went to them and said that they had to leave Bailey and the others. Kate and Michaela weren't sure why, but then they saw the others jump into a car and drive off without them.

"So what do we do now?" asked Kate.
"We walk," Ben replied.
None of them really liked the idea of walking, but Ben knew that they were actually really close to the safe place.

As they continued on their way, they heard a loud noise behind them, and that was the sound of a humaning boat heading their direction. The boat drove above them just as Ben yelled for Kate and Michaela to run as fast as they could. Ben looked up again after a while of running and noticed the boat begin to slow down.

"Come on, we're nearly there, everything has to go to plan," yelled Ben.

Kate and Michaela looked at each other, wondering if they were ever going to make it to the safe place, and continued anyway as they had nowhere else to go. But then it occurred to them.

They were following a guy that appeared from the shadows of an abandoned house, telling them that they should travel with him, and was now getting them to follow him, running after a boat that resembled the one that captured hundreds of people with a giant net, and this was supposed to be where a safe place was. Then that's when they stopped running, and realised this may have all been a trap.

Kate then ran closer to Ben and knew that it would be hard to get him to say anything if he was like Bailey. She pulled out Tara's knife she picked up in the rubbish, ran up to him, and held it against his neck. After everything she had experienced so far, death became a normal thing, an accepted thing, maybe even a necessary thing.

"Ben, tell us the truth. Why do we need to follow you to the safe place?" asked Kate.

"Wait a minute Kate. Don't do anything you're going to regret," stammered Ben.

"Yeah, what are you doing Kate, he's our friend," said Michaela.

"Maybe not. A friend would tell us the truth and he hasn't done that yet. I'm doing this to ensure our survival. You said it yourself Michaela. We're living in a new world, and I think I just realised that survival is key, whether or not the decisions made are adequate or not."

Michaela didn't know what to do as Kate said, "Just tell us why we're needed and where we're actually going, and I'll let you go, okay."

Then as Ben sighed, he knew it was about time he told them the truth.

"Okay, I'll tell you both the truth. You deserve it after what you've been through. Back when I first found a time machine with the others, you guys ran to us and said that I had to go back in time and meet you two, only to bring both of you back here. I wasn't sure about it at first, but time seemed to be falling apart around me so I decided to go back in time and trust I was being told the truth.

You both handed me a map of where I had to go and that's what I've been following the whole time. I was told that this had to happen for the time loop to continue.

If you guys don't come and decide not to meet my past self. Do not get him convinced in going back to the past, and fail to give him the map back here, you'll die. Either in the town of the hungry-ones or what happened with the humaning net and so on. If you don't convince my past self to go to the past, you'll both die, breaking the time loop, and destroy all of time. Ending all life. That's why you need to follow me right now."

"So there isn't a safe place then?" asked Kate.

"Not really. It's as safe as any other place though. But if you don't do what I said before, time will break, and you'll all die."

"Wait, what is the point of this whole loop thing anyway? What actually started the loop? Why were we specifically needed and not anyone else, when was the time machine invented and who made it? What is going on?" asked Kate.

"I really don't know the answer to any of those questions. You're just going to have to trust that I know what I'm doing and go along with it, because if we don't do this, time will shatter... and we'll all most likely disappear from existence."

Ben continued, "So it's your choice now. You will now decide whether we all live, or die. Make the right decision if you can."

Kate moved the knife away from Ben's neck as she realised she had made a mistake.

Then Ben continued to run after the boat. Soon Michaela looked over at Kate as she was annoyed at Ben for lying, but kind of understood why he did it and followed Ben. Then as Kate followed from behind, she hoped that she'd made the right decision.

They were catching up to the boat when Ben waved for Kate and Michaela to hide behind some trees as three giant sharks appeared with spears in their hands and walking in separate directions. One was heading the way Ben, Kate and Michaela were heading (as planned), one was heading in a different direction away from everyone, and the third one headed in a different direction as well.

Kate and Michaela immediately ran around the tree to hide while Ben followed. As he hid, he turned back and saw a car heading towards them, and had an idea who would be in it, and yes, Darian, Tom, and two other people appeared.

"Hey Ben, sorry about what I did just before, it was uncalled for," said Kate.

"Don't worry about it. This has been a rough couple of days, but I am going to be weary around you still just in case."

Then as Kate felt more ashamed, Michaela tried to comfort her, even though she wasn't sure what to think of this.

Tom had switched drivers with Darian as he had a good rest and needed to make sure they were going in the right direction. The car stopped in front of Ben, Kate and Michaela. Then Tom rolled down his window and said, "Ben, let's get out of here."
Tom had already told the others what the plan was and they agreed to it so they hopped out of the car.

Ben was about to head off, when he remembered something important.

"Michaela, make sure you hand these car keys to my past self when you see him with the time machine. This is crucial for the loop to continue properly."
Ben handed Michaela the car keys, turned around and ran towards the car to jump in it.

"Wait, where are you guys going!" yelled Michaela.
"Don't worry, we'll be back soon."
"We need to stay hidden so that our past selves don't see us. Just please make sure that all of you meet our past selves, and convince them to go to the past as well," said Ben.
"What, how can we do that!" yelled Michaela.
"You'll work it out, and when it's done, we'll meet up with all of you when our past selves are gone."

Then Ben and Tom shut their doors and drove off. Everyone left behind kind of knew what they had to do next.
They had to continue the loop.

The World Above
New Frontier
Chapter 31
The Chase

Meanwhile, back with Ben, Tom, Adam, Seth and Josh…
They could all breathe properly now so no one had to travel
close together or on top of Adam's hands. They all walked
away from the battered drone behind them not really knowing
what to do. They had escaped back to the world below, and
there was nothing they really needed to do then as they had
succeeded on the return back.

Ben and Tom wanted to find their family while Adam
followed from behind. In the future, Seth was meant to run to
a building with Jared, Nick, Regen, Josh, Rusheel and Bailey,
but the future may be at risk from never happening as the only
person alive in that group was Josh… so Seth decided to stay
with him.

As Ben was wandering around, he was thinking about what
Tom, his brother said about the fish. Then he thought about all
of the fish that helped them out throughout their entire journey
back to The World Below and realised that maybe all fish
weren't bad at all. They were all just being stereotyped. He
was starting to accept that the fish did kind of act like people,
but he still wasn't sure if that made things better or not since
most people were just as bad as the fish when humans were
the dominant species in The World Above.

Seth decided to stay with Ben, Tom and Adam as he did visit them from the future. Then as they walked over to Josh, they felt a sudden shake in the ground. Josh was facing the approaching thing and immediately turned back in panic as a giant spear hunting shark was in front with two other sharks going in different directions away from them.

In fright, they all immediately started to run away from the shark as it suddenly occurred to Seth that a time machine was involved the entire time. Someone was using one and was traveling around teleporting them to different places and making objects appear if needed. The blue circles must have represented time travel being used the entire time and if that was the case, someone from this group had been a time traveller from the start because they were the only people that saw it all happen, and that's when he realised he was the time traveller, and he had to find another time machine, before a spear hunting shark shot him.

As Ben started his run away from the shark, a blue aura started to surround him once again, causing everyone to freeze in time once more as Ben looked around and saw Beth in front of him.

"Oh, hey Beth, I haven't seen you in a while, but what advice…"

"Stop, stop, stop. I'm so sorry about everything I've done so far. I, I didn't mean it. I was brainwashed by Jabnmine, you, you have to believe me."

"What are you talking about Beth, and who's Jabnmine?"

"No time to explain that rig, rig, right now. Just know that you hav, hav, have to let everyone die."

"Wait what."

"I have no tim, tim, time to explain why, but when you rea, reac, reach the time machine, let everyone die an, an, and everything will go back to nor, nor, normal.

"Beth, what's wrong with your voice. Are you okay?" asked Ben.

"Everything's not o, o, okay. Not unless you le, le, let everyone die. Oh and my names no, no, not Beth. My na, na, name is actually A, A, Am, Da, A, Madr. Jst dn't lsen to anyhng els I syyyy. Hey, how's it going? Ignore what I was saying before, I guaranteed it won't happen again," Beth cheerfully said.

"Um, what happened to you just then," asked Ben.

"I think I was struggling to stay in the time room and it was messing up my speaking, but I've fixed the problem and you won't hear any more of that nonsense anymore," replied Beth.

"Okay, why are you here then?" asked Ben.

"I just wanted to tell you to press the middle button between two arrows on the time machine to allow you to save everyone from being shot," answered Beth.

"Wait a minute, you just told me to let everyone die though."

"Seriously. Were you really going to just let everyone die because my voice was muddled up."

"I don't really know anymore."

"Look, letting everyone die would be bad because you're going to need as many people as you can gather for the future and without them, the loop would break and ultimately destroy time."

"Oh, right, uh what's happening in the future?" asked Ben.

"The war, the war for the world above, and if you let everyone die, you will lose the war, and everyone will suffer for

eternity. Just make sure you save everyone, and everything can become the way it should be, forever.
Anyway, I need to go now so, see ya later."
Then as Beth disappeared and Ben was placed back into reality again, he remembered the shark and continued to run, not knowing what he should do next.

Seth continued to run with everyone else when he noticed some kind of lab in front of them. A strange random out of place lab. They all saw it as a place to hide and ran towards it. The shark pointed the spear gun at Josh as he continued his run behind everyone. He looked behind and realised the shark was aiming the spear gun at him. He started to try and sidestep the spear by jumping from one side to the other, but it was futile in the end as the shark managed to shoot him dead on.

Ben, Tom, Seth and Adam continued their run when they noticed the shark lock in another spear and start to aim it at Tom as everyone was a little further in front of him. Tom tried to try and sidestep the spear when it pulled the trigger and fired it at Tom. With quick reflexes though, Tom's robot arm managed to grab the spear mid-air, spin in a circle, and throw it away from him and into the leg of the other shark further from him, making the shark swim to the surface. Then as Tom was just realising what he did, the shark aimed another spear at Tom and fired it at him, causing a dust cloud to emerge from the hit.

The shark saw this as just a sport as that's what most other sharks and fish did. It only had done this a couple of times before and it was completely legal for him to do this as he knew he could only get a certain amount of humans that looked the right size, and that was perfectly okay as humans didn't really think about much anyway. Their only goal was purely to survive and reproduce and nothing else really as they weren't as intellectually developed as the sharks and fish.

The shark also thought that humans didn't even seem to show any signs of remorse when others got killed. Instead, they just ran away from the area as fast as they could. It couldn't be from fear though, or maybe it was. Meh, that didn't matter. There were plenty of humans around anyway and since they all looked the same, none of them would notice when other humans were gone because if we couldn't see a difference between them, surely they couldn't either. That is exactly what the shark thought when doing this.

A shark was about to find Darian, Amanda, Michaela, Kate and Shane when the spear Tom threw, sailed into the sharks' leg, causing it to swim to the surface.
Darian looked in front of her hiding spot realising that the rest of the guys weren't going to make it by themselves and that Tom stopped a shark from finding them.

Kate and Michaela were trying to work out how they were going to convince Ben to go to the past especially after what had happened before, while Amanda and Shane were wondering where they were going to go once it was all over. Then it occurred to Darian that there were only three guys left, and that they were going to die. They had to do something to help them out.

After a quick talk, all of them started their run towards the shark as it placed its next spear inside the gun and aimed it at Seth. The shark was just about to fire it when he noticed some blood floating around and realised it was blood from his mate's leg that was caused by the spear the human somehow threw. And that just caused the shark to get even angrier. Then just as he was about to aim at Seth again, a bunch of humans appeared in front of him.

Kate and the others ran along as fast as they could, gave a big leap, managed to jump really high and hover to the ground. They couldn't believe they could jump so high as they leaped over the shark, but the shark noticed them and prepared another spear to aim. They were all about to land when the shark shot Michaela mid-air right as she vanished. The rest of them landed while the shark prepared its next spear and aimed it.

They had almost reached the entrance of the lab when the shark had properly aimed the next spear at Shane and fired it. The spear flew through the air and directly shot Shane, just as he vanished into a cloud of dust. Then as Amanda shed a tear, they all ran into the building to hide away, but they knew that it couldn't have been over yet. Seth knew that there had to be a time machine in there somewhere. He just needed to find it.

The shark walked towards the lab and instead of just turning away, it decided to try and get the rest of them by grabbing the roof of the lab and ripping it open to reveal where everyone was. Then it immediately pulled out its spear gun and started to aim it again at Darian.

Everyone was getting desperate and no one knew where to go until Adam yelled, "Follow me guys!"

The voice in Adams' head was once again trying to tell him where to go as everyone followed from behind. The shark had properly aimed the spear and shot Darian as she vanished into the ground. Then Adam yelled "All we have to do is to keep going down this corridor, turn right, and enter the fourth door on the left. Then the shark clicked in another spear, aimed it at Adam, and shot him. When Adam vanished from getting shot, a blue aura appeared around him as a cloud of darkness formed in that area when everyone ran through it. Then when the shark clicked in another spear, the dark cloud vanished.

Kate, Seth, Amanda and Ben were the only survivors left as they proceeded to the end of the corridor and turned right, just as the shark clicked in another spear, aimed it properly once again, and without hesitation, fired it at Kate. She vanished as the spear smashed into the ground. Seth counted the doors they passed and the three of them entered the fourth door on the left, only to see the time machine in a glass case with complicated technology around it. Then the shark clicked in another spear, aimed it at them, and just as Seth picked up a rock and threw it at the glass, the spear went through him, making him vanish.

Amanda and Ben were the only ones left as they both ran to the time machine to work out what to do with it. Then as they were thinking about it, the shark clicked in another spear and aimed it at them. Ben picked it up, found a number code, and immediately set it to go 5 minutes into the past and away from the area. Then clicked the red button and felt his body start to feel weird. Amanda was trying to work out what she could do to help when the shark fired the spear towards her.

Ben realised this and pushed her away, making her start to get pulled into the time machine. The spear ended up going through Ben's body instead of Amanda's, but not harming him as he was being twisted into the vortex. The spear smashed through the stand holding up the time machine making it fall as Amanda also started to feel weird. When she saw it falling, she immediately grabbed it, making it also get affected and follow them into the vortex. Ben and Amanda were melting and disappearing as the time machine followed from behind.

The shark clicked in another spear, but decided not to fire another one as he watched the two of them spinning in circles and eventually disappear into a blue mist, with the time machine following them from behind.
They had both completely vanished, leaving the shark really confused. What confused him more was that all the other humans he shot were gone as well.

He picked up all of its spears only to find not a single person attached to any of them. Then in fear, anger and disbelief, it immediately went to swim up to the surface to see how its mate was going. Soon the third shark swam up as well, but none of them were sure about what had happened, and they just headed home to try and forget about the entire trip.

The World Above
New Frontier
Chapter 32
The Time machine

Ben and Amanda flew through the time vortex with blue, green and yellow spirals surrounding them completely. Their bodies looked like spirals spinning around each other as none of them knew where they were going five minutes into the past. Then as they looked forward into the vortex, it started to shape into a bit of a clock that was spinning into itself as the two of them flew into it, not knowing what would happen to them.

Ben reappeared with Amanda appearing next to him, and the time machine appearing in her arms. They both looked around wondering where they were as Ben looked across to Amanda wondering if he had seen her before. She kind of reminded him of Beth a little and that's when Ben asked her what her name was and she answered, "Oh, my names Amanda, thanks for saving me back there, you know, when you pushed me away from the spear." Then Ben replied, "Oh yeah, just reflexes, by the way my names Ben, nice to meet you." They both kind of smiled at each other when they saw something from the corners of their eye. It was their past selves.

Amanda saw the group she was with and noticed Tom drive off with Ben in a different direction. Ben saw his group in the distance walking away from the battered drone wandering around. Then as the group looked behind them, they noticed the boat appear above with three sharks entering their world, when one shark headed towards Amanda's group in front of them, the other shark started to head towards Ben's group. The third shark went in a completely different direction, and that was towards Ben and Amanda.

Ben and Amanda immediately ran behind a rock to try not to get seen by the shark when Ben saw his past self-hanging with his brother and the others. Then he watched them all turn away and get chased by the shark throwing spears at them. Amanda grabbed his wrist as she pulled him to the other side of the rock where the shark continued to search the area for any humans. Then as Ben turned back to his group, he watched in sadness as he saw Josh get shot by a spear without any hesitation.

Then when he saw his brother throw the spear into the other shark's leg, the spear caused the shark to not even find Amanda's group. The shark had swum up to the surface in pain just as Tom was pushed into the ground from the second spear fired at him. Watching his brother die really made him think about whether or not the fish were their villains. And he realised that they were.

It didn't matter that they acted human. The fish had a mindset that killing humans was perfectly fine, and after watching everyone he knew get shot by one, he continued to hate the fish. He knew that the fish would always be their enemy. And nothing could change that.

He looked back at the time machine as he searched through all the buttons. As they both ran around the rock to hide from the shark, Amanda saw her group running towards the other shark as well, watching Michaela get shot. The weird thing was that there weren't any dead bodies around the spears that were shot. Then as Ben looked closely, he noticed a strange blue light speeding to everyone just before they died.

Ben wasn't sure what the blue aura was, but he had a feeling it involved the time machine. He looked over at Amanda to talk about that with her when the shark picked up the rock they were hiding behind and saw them. The shark immediately pulled out his spear as Ben and Amanda ran behind a tree, just as the spear was shot. They hid behind the tree as the spear flew through it, but got jammed halfway, just missing Ben.

Amanda grabbed the time machine and set it to four minutes into the past when the shark stepped forward towards them with another spear getting clicked in. She pushed the red button and activated it. While Ben was getting over nearly getting shot, Amanda grabbed him and held onto the time machine to allow both of them to disappear into the vortex. The shark had already set up the spear gun and shot it at them just as they vanished, leaving the shark confused about where they went.

Ben and Amanda travelled through the vortex once again with blurred blue, green and yellow colours spinning around them. Then the clock like thing in the end spun them back in time again.
They both reappeared, hoping they weren't near their past selves and in relief, they weren't. They had appeared right under the boat. Looking forward, they saw their past selves wondering where they had ended up. Then they looked further and saw their other past selves as well.

As they saw the three sharks do their thing, Amanda noticed the car Ben and Tom were driving away with as they parked the car up ahead and got out. Future Ben looked at Amanda and tried to hide away. Future Ben and his brother found a hiding place behind the car before the present Ben saw them.

Amanda decided to leave the future versions of Ben and Tom alone as she turned back to the present Ben to see him examining the Time Machine. Ben wasn't sure how the time machine worked, but continued to look it over when he found three buttons on the opposite side from the red one.

There was an arrow pointing to the left, one pointing to the right, and the middle one was just a circle with a blue dot on it, and as Ben debated with himself on what to do next, he touched the middle blue dot to see what would happen. The blue dot started to lift up and become a button. The sharks were only just landing when both Ben and Amanda pushed the blue button.
A blue aura surrounded them as they looked around seeing everything unfold. Ben pushed the arrow pointing to the left and made time slow down. Everyone and everything started to move really slowly all of a sudden. Then as they started to walk to the others, they were also walking in slow motion too. At first, they were confused about this but figured they were now in a slow-paced world and wondered if they could travel through the vortex while time was slow.

The shark was clicking in its first spear when Ben and Amanda pushed the red button on the time machine, and the blurred colours of blue, green and yellow passed through them. Instead of floating in a vortex, they were able to walk around. Then as the two of them held onto the time machine, (not knowing what would happen if they let go) they started to walk over to the others. The shark had shot its first spear and as it went through the air, Ben and Amanda ran to Josh as he ran in slow motion.

Ben was going to let everyone die, since that was what Beth originally instructed him to do, but he just couldn't justify that choice. He also wanted to protect his mates from the villainess sharks so when the spear was getting closer to Josh, Ben and Amanda used their spare arms to grab Josh and pull him into the time room, making the spear just miss him and leave blue spinning circles in the area.

As Josh got pulled into the time room, Ben and Amanda made sure they still had a hold of him so he wasn't lost in the vortex, and so the blue aura surrounded him as well. Josh had many questions of how Ben was in two places at once and who Amanda was. They just told him they'd answer his questions later and that they were busy saving everyone. Josh didn't really want to argue with them as they stopped him from getting shot, but he was still confused.

When Josh had calmed down, the three of them looked ahead and saw Tom as he made it more difficult for them to save him. Tom continually sidestepped away from them as the shark aimed the spear at him and fired it. The spear sailed through the air as it flew through Josh and between Ben and Amanda, just as Toms robot arm grabbed the spear, spun it around and threw it at the other shark. Then because Tom had stopped moving, the shark aimed up another spear at Tom and fired it, just as Ben and Amanda grabbed him and pulled him in.

Ben and Amanda tried to keep Tom calm and okay as Josh hung on to keep them both from falling out of the time room.

Ben and Amanda looked around and noticed the next spear get aimed at Seth until the shark noticed blood appear near him.

"Seriously what is going on Josh, how did you get here?"
"I don't know, the spear nearly got me before I appeared here because of Ben and this other person."
"Don't worry guys, we'll explain everything shortly, but for now we need to save people." Then just as Ben said that, Amanda looked up and yelled "Ben, look up!" and saw Michaela mid-air just as the next spear got clicked in and aimed at her. Amanda immediately jumped up as Ben followed behind. Then as she grabbed Michaela's leg, Michaela got pulled into the time room just before the spear got her.

The three of them landed on the ground as Ben looked back and saw his past self behind a tree looking at them. All his past self could see was a blurry blue light. Another spear was heading for Shane as he was running to the lab when the spear was fired at him. Amanda immediately grabbed him and pulled him into the time room as well, just before the spear slid through his chest.

Everyone had managed to run into the lab as Josh and Tom were trying to calm Michaela and Shane down. Then as they were about to enter the lab, Ben looked up and saw the shark push his hands under the roof of the lab, and tear it off. The shark immediately threw it away and pulled out its spear gun. Everyone in the time room followed the others into the lab. Immediately, the shark clicked in another spear and aimed it at Darian until he fired it. Everyone had already run into the lab when they saw the spear heading towards Darian as

Amanda reached out and grabbed her. Then just before the spear got her, Ben slowed down time even more, which allowed Darian to narrowly get pulled into the time room, but now the place was getting more crowded and the blue blur was starting to get more noticeable. The time room did have a limit to how much people could fit in it and slowly it was starting to rip apart.

Time sped up at a normal pace again so the time room could stay intact, but it was ripping apart even more as darkness seeped into it. The darkness spread across the bottom of the time room as it started to consume everyone, making the back of the room start to open up. The shark aimed its next spear at Adam as Ben and Amanda attempted to pull him in. As Adam was being pulled in, he seemed to be struggling a lot more since he didn't seem to want to be pulled in. Then as the darkness of the void was somehow escaping the time room and into reality, the spirit within Adam gave up and let everyone pull him in.

The spear was shot at Adam and missed him, but the shark didn't know that because there was a strange dark mist surrounding the area. The dark mist of the void eventually vanished and the shark was now ready to fire another spear at Kate. Ben and Amanda realised that the time room wasn't able to fit too many people anymore as they struggled to pull Kate in. Then just as the spear was shot, Ben and Amanda tried the best they could, pushing everyone in the time room close together and pulled her in. The spear only just missed her, but there was no way they'd be able to fit anyone else inside.

The darkness continued to spread up everyone's bodies, making them feel weak and sick including Ben and Amanda. No one knew this, but because they were in a vortex, they weren't in reality anymore, and the void was trying to consume everyone in the time room. Everyone was starting to go through the first stage of death when Amanda yelled out that they all had to go now. She set the time machine to go five minutes into the future when the shark was clicking in another spear to shoot Seth.

Amanda pushed the red button and because everyone was grabbing onto each other, they were all getting pulled into the time machine. Kate and Adam were near the back and they felt the worst from the voids touch. Then as Kate let go, her body was half in the void when Adam grabbed her wrist. The time machine was making everyone swirl around it. Then Adam became part of it and continued to pull Kate out of the void as well. Ben wasn't fully twisted into the spirals as Seth was still unsafe. Then the shark let the spear fly.

Everyone was getting pulled into the time machine away from the darkness that had nearly taken over the whole room when Ben reached out and grabbed Seth's wrist, and pulled him in. As he got pulled in, Ben was a little late and the spear went through a bit of Seth's shirt. Ben was pulled into the vortex as Seth also started to follow him when Seth grabbed the time machine and disappeared into the vortex away from the time room that had completely become smothered by the void. The past versions of Amanda and Ben made it to the time machine and escaped, just before the spear got them, and then it all continued to repeat again.

Everyone travelled through the vortex not knowing where they were going as the blurred colours of blue, green and yellow surrounded them. Then at the end, a clock soon appeared and as it started to spin into itself, everyone got pulled into it, only to re-emerge five minutes into the future.

Everyone was confused about the time machine as they appeared and started to ask Amanda and Ben all about it. Eventually, Seth did a massive high pitched whistle causing everyone to stop talking. Kate was able to move around properly again as she wasn't in the void long enough to harm her for life, but she still felt a little ill.

As Ben cupped his ears, a blue aura started to surround him as Beth emerged, saying, "Great job Ben, you did it. Everyone is alive and we're one step closer to making the world perfect."
"Mhmm, you mean, make the world normal right."
"Sure, if that's what you think. Anyway, I don't think you'll really need me anymore as you seem to be good at making the right decisions so anyway, seeya la…" Beth seemed to be uncontrollably shaking as she yelled "No, no, no, no. Ben how could you do this. You, you've doomed the world forever now. Why didn't you listen to me and let everyone die? It's all over now. Because of this, Jabnmine will never get defea… uh, this time room isn't as good as it used to be. Don't worry. You made the right decision. I'm just going to go now before I accidentally say anything incorrectly incorrect again. Seeya."

As Ben stood in shock the whole time not knowing what to say or think, Beth disappeared and the blue aura vanished, leaving Ben back in reality again. He wasn't sure how he could describe Beth to everyone else, but started to question what had happened since he was sure that he had made the right decision. He just couldn't justify letting everyone die.

The World Above
The New Frontier
Chapter 33
Continuing the loop

Michaela walked up to Kate and reminded her about that thing where Ben had to go to the past. Darian also needed to go to Tom and convince him to go to the past as well. Even though those versions of Ben and Tom saw them as strangers.

"Alright guys, now that everyone is quiet, let's let our time travelling friends tell us what happened and then they'll answer other questions afterwards."

The shark's boat had driven off ages ago with very confused sharks, which meant that none of the group were in any danger of getting shot.
Amanda and Ben tried to give a good description to explain what had happened to them and as everyone was starting to understand and accept it, it still left everyone a little confused.

"Alright, is there anyone that wants to ask us something?" asked Ben.
"Yep, can you go back in time to make sure our past selves get here?" asked Michaela.
"Wait, what did you just ask?"
"Alright, a few days ago, your past self-appeared and helped us get here. We know it's hard to believe, but it has to be done to continue the loop," said Kate.
"So have you got a map of how to get you guys back here or even a description of where I'll end up?" asked Ben.

"Yep, your future-self handed us this. It's a map that will lead you back here with us."

"Why is there a gap in the path we're meant to go along?"

"I think that's when we teleport somewhere. Anyway, I think you have to go soon."

"Wait a minute, I don't know you guys, what if I end up in the middle of nowhere and stranded?"

Tom was just about to say, "Then you'll have a map to get back," to Ben, but figured that wasn't necessary. It just didn't seem possible to be positive at the moment.

Ben looked at Tom, thinking that he might say something about the map when glowing cracks started to form in the ground around them as time was falling apart.

"So all I have to do is follow the map?" asked Ben.

"Yep, and you have to find a way to get our past selves to follow you. Just warning, it may be difficult to get us to come with you without these. This is the keys to the first car we drove to get out of the town and you can use this to get us to go with you," said Michaela.

Michaela handed the keys over to Ben and went over to Amanda to set the time machine to where he had to go. Then Darian ran to him and yelled, "Um before you go, my names Darian, and please remember to throw the shield to me when you see my past self. It's really important that you do that. I even have a version of it with me to hand back to your future self."

"Mhmm okay then, I think I will remember who you are when I see you, and pass you the shield, I guess." Then as Ben acknowledged what Darian said, he pushed the red button and went back in time without holding the time machine so it didn't follow him.

The glowing cracks continued to spread wider even when Ben disappeared and that made Seth realise this may have been how time would shatter. This was all because the future wasn't able to happen anymore. The glowing cracks were spreading closer to everyone when Darian went up to Tom and said that he had to go back in time as well. She handed Tom a map of how to get back there and even though he was confused, he decided to go.

He was told about the location to meet her at and what he had to do to get to her. Then as he agreed to it and was able to remember her face, Darian pushed in the coordinates and let Tom push the red button to get sent to the past. Tom was told how he would rescue her, but he wasn't even sure if he could drive like that. Then he thought he'd find out soon and had just accepted his fate.

The glowing cracks were opening up in a specific area when darkness started to form out of it, and that was when Seth accepted what was going to happen and how it was all his fault. Then as Adam, Kate, Michaela, Shane, Josh and Amanda looked over the glowing cracks, more darkness was spreading out of it everywhere around everyone's ankles.

As this happened, a car pulled up to them with Ben and Tom jumping out of it running over to everyone. Kate, Michaela and Darian realised that the loop worked and that they didn't stuff everything up, but only made them wonder why reality seemed to be falling apart. Then as Ben noticed the dark mist causing everyone to suffer the first stage of death, he saw a hand in the glowing cracks. Then as he ran in first to help pull the hand out. He didn't know why he did it. But he did it anyway.

As Ben ran to the hand, Tom was stunned over how the mist was slowly causing everyone to fall to the ground as a cry for help was called within the glowing cracks.

Then as Ben reached into it, he pulled back on the hand as the whole arm was appearing and started to pull the person out. Then he realised he was slowly getting pulled in. He was slipping into the glowing cracks as well when Kate knew how to redeem herself. She had almost completed the first stage of death as she crawled from behind with glowing cracks forming beneath her.

Ben's legs had fallen into the glowing cracks as Kate used all her remaining strength to pull Ben out. Then since he was pulled out. Tom reached his robot arm and used its strength to help pull the person within the golden cracks out as well.

Everyone else fell to the ground and went through the second stage of death as blue sparks were appearing everywhere. Then Ben managed to pull a person's head out of the darkness just as Kate collapsed to the ground. With a final burst of strength, Ben and Tom pulled the person out of the glowing cracks just as they both felt weak and fell to the ground to suffer the second stage of death.

As everyone was about to go through the third stage of death, the darkness started to disappear back into the glowing cracks since the person had been pulled out. When the guy was fully pulled out, he collapsed to the ground and rested with everyone else as they all tried to recover from being in the darkness for that long.

Eventually, everyone started to get up and recovered quickly. They weren't actually in the void so they weren't hit with the full effects. Then as everyone looked at the person that had been pulled out, most people didn't even know who he was.

It turned out that the glowing cracks weren't reality falling apart, but it was someone returning from the void. And when Seth saw the guy's face, he knew exactly who it was and stood back, telling everyone else to step away as well. Adam also saw the face and instantly recalled who it was as well as it was the person who became an evil spirit trying to consume everyone's souls. The person they had saved, was Nick.

The World Above
New Frontier
Chapter 34
Those that Returned

As Seth and Adam were trying to back everyone away from Nick, a thought occurred to Seth as Nick was actually still needed in the future so he could run with everyone to the building.

Nick started to get up as he struggled to do anything. With positive emotions and feelings been temporarily removed, he was slowly recovering his memories of how to walk, talk and recall past events. He was struggling a lot as he had spent some time in the void and wasn't really sure who he even was.

As his memories were returning, he tried to stand up straight. Then looking around, seemed confused about where he was as he looked himself over and realised he had his body back, but wasn't sure why he was glad he had his body back. Then all of his original memories returned including the ones involving him as an evil spirit.

As he was able to walk properly again, Seth walked up to him, unsure of what he had to do next since Nick appeared red-faced and tired. Nick said, "I'm so sorry about everything I did in the past. I, I was brainless and couldn't think properly. I was so desperate. It seemed like my only option at the time. But I'm sorry for everything I did."

Adam was also listening. Then when Adam got closer to Nick, the spirit within him realised Nick had escaped the void somehow. Immediately the spirit gained full control over Adam again since he wanted to send Nick back to where he belonged. Then as Adam's eyes turned backwards, he realised what was happening and knew that he had to take back control of himself. Nick had apologised and Seth felt obligated to trust him in order to continue the loop.

"Why are you stopping me from sending Nick back to where he belongs. Don't you remember what he tried to do to all of us?" asked the spirit.
"Yes, I remember what he did. I don't know what you did to him last time, but I know that you shouldn't do it again," answered Adam.
"Ah, why am I even talking to you? I possessed you so I can do whatever I want."
"No. He apologised, and I won't let you gain control over me again."
Then as the spirit was forcefully trying to separate itself from Adam to attack Nick once again, Adam managed to use all of his strength to hold the spirit back. As this happened, Josh was looking at him doing this and had no idea what was going on. That was until he saw the outline of the spirit trying to pull itself out of Adam.

When Darian saw Ben, she decided to throw him back his shield and thanked him for it since it turned out really helpful in the end.
As Ben and Tom told everyone briefly what had happened to them, another car pulled up to them with Rusheel, Jared, Bailey, Regen and Seth's past self in it.
Seth noticed this and that's when he turned back to Nick and said, "So you really are apologising for what you did and that your fine?"

"Yes, I am. After being in the void for as long as I was, I realised that having no positive feelings or emotions was the worst part of the void and that I wanted to experience them again by doing good things for others. I want to be remembered as a good person."

"Then maybe you can do something for me," said Seth. Rusheel ran out of the car, while everyone else stayed back with Seth's past self to keep him from leaving too. They were all amazed and glad that everyone was okay. Then they saw Seth walking Nick over to Rusheel saying that he was safe now.
Rusheel still didn't trust Nick even after some talking, but eventually accepted that Nick was still necessary for the future.

Adam was still trying to hold back the spirits attack until he saw Rusheel talking to Nick once again. The spirit looked back and saw a car full of everyone that had supposedly died. Then as the spirit thought about this, he realised that he was gaining some once erased memories. Memories containing an endless loop involving Nick. Even though he had a feeling that the loop was bad news, part of it knew that it was necessary.

Soon Nick started to head to the car as Rusheel walked over to Seth and asked him what they needed to do then. Seth answered that as long as they did what his past self-wanted to do, everyone would be okay, live to meet the future, and that none of them could die no matter what. Rusheel agreed to this, but even though he was curious about why they were all needed in the future, he decided not to question it. Then Adam's spirit relaxed and gave Adam full control once again.

The spirit was impressed with Adam's mental strength and realised he may have accidentally possessed a worthy person to defeat something powerful. He couldn't quite work out what that powerful being was though since everything still seemed like a mystery.

Rusheel headed back to the car quickly as Seth's past self was starting the car and everyone wanted to go. Then Seth looked over at Josh and realised he was meant to hang with his past self as well to continue the loop. So Seth walked up to him and asked Josh to go hang out with them instead for important time travel reasons.

Josh replied with, "Um sure, but why do I have to go with them? Actually, since Nick is going with them, I don't think I want to go because of what he did to me."
"Look, he's a changed person; you'll be fine, just go over there and see for yourself."
"No, I think I'm fine being here with you guys."
Then when Seth was trying to think of other ways to convince Josh, spinning circles appeared around his head making him believe it was necessary to leave the group, causing him to say, "Actually, Nick seems kind of safe so I guess that I might as well hang out with those guys. Good idea Seth."

Seth wasn't sure what changed Josh's mind, but let it happen anyway as he watched Josh jump into the seven seated car with everyone else. One reason Josh joined the group though was simply because of Adam. There was something weird happening to him. Josh just couldn't work out what it was. Everyone seemed to be okay with Nick and Josh hanging with them immediately as well. The spinning circles surrounding their heads couldn't have been a cause for it though, Seth thought.

Then as the guys drove off with the car, Seth knew that somehow everyone needed for the future had made it in one piece. He only hoped that they'd be there to run to the time machine and continue that loop.

Tom also noticed the car there and saw everyone within it. He seemed surprised as everyone who had died seemed to still be alive for some reason. Then as he noticed Bailey chatting with everyone in the car, he knew that it was still possible for positivity to arise in this situation.

Positivity could never be forced. It had to be naturally developed. It was never lost. It just wasn't fully discovered. Now that Tom truly believed that again, he knew what he could do to help everyone suffering during this. He just had to continue believing that the world could be back to normal. That everyone that had died didn't need to remain dead. That he always needed to be hopeful that things could get better. This was how he'd stay positive. He had to stay with the others, fix the world, and was now more determined to do so than ever before.

As this was all happening, something occurred to Adam as he realised the dream he had back in the human tank was partially coming true since the clocks that surrounded him must have represented time travel being used. The spirit that tried to escape must have represented the spirit within him, but he wasn't sure with any of the other things yet as he didn't know what the three blue beings that surrounded him were, or even why vines were wrapping around him. He didn't even know what the vine monster was, yet it was in his vision, and somehow would be connected to his future.

Then as Adam tried to work things out, Amanda had run up to Ben being really glad that he had made it back and hugged him.
After Ben and Amanda talked for a bit, Ben wandered over to Kate and asked if she trusted him, and when Kate looked forward towards him, she knew that he had always been twisting the truth a little in order to help her and Michaela survive. After that, they knew that they could count on each other again and help each other out if needed.

Ben had thought about whether or not fish were villains and decided to agree that after he'd witness some fish be really helpful, and some humans act really bad. He knew that every being involved in this, whether or not they were a fish or human were all individual subjective thinkers who had their own beliefs about the situation.

The fish were doing everything that humans once did, but that meant that there were also other fish acting to protect air life as well and restore it. Some fish probably didn't even think they were doing anything wrong the whole time since they seemed to be individuals that did stupid things as well, such as throwing rocks at frozen layers of air... which didn't seem possible, but was apparently real according to Tom. Fish weren't the enemy, and humans weren't the enemy either. The being who switched the worlds was the enemy, and it had to be his main focus for now on.

As the group formed around the time machine, Amanda wandered over to Ben and stood next to him, noticing who was still with them. Kate, Michaela, Seth, Adam, Tom, Darian and Shane were still there, and as they all looked to Ben and Amanda who had the time machine, a question stood in everyone's minds.

Now that they had the time machine, and they could go where ever or whenever they wanted, what were they supposed to do now?

The World Above
New Frontier
Chapter 35
Time-Correction-Squares

As everyone stood in a group, Seth started to explain the Time-Correction-Squares a little better.

"Time-Correction-Squares were spreading all over the world spreading over anything and anyone. The more it spread, the faster it got, and the further it sent things back in time. No one, no matter how fast you were, could escape them as they would spread far enough that different parts of the Time-Correction-Squares would be in different time periods. Time-Correction-Squares would send things months, to years, to decades, to centuries into the past until they disappeared from existence."

"Time-Correction-Squares would spread up buildings and over anyone inside it. They had already started to emerge around historical things and spread so far back that even the historical things started to get blocky. The pyramids were consumed by them and so was the Sphinx as it even got its nose re-created onto it. Paintings from museums like the Louvre started to disappear into blocks including the Mona Lisa. The Eiffel Tower completely collapsed into a bunch of cubes followed by everyone around it."

Seth continued with, "In Australia, even Uluru started to collapse into a bunch of cubic blocks and replaced with giant footprints covering it with giant pieces of rubbish smothering most aspects of the area.

People would disappear from existence when they touched the squares and got sent so far back that their late relatives never met, and even if they did meet, the person might have been born at a different time or lived in different conditions, making them become a different person.

Then Seth added on, "The area I ran through to get to the time machine was one of the only places not affected by the Time-Correction-Squares. It was too late to do anything as everything was gone.

That's why I used the time machine to go to the past.

I had to have more time to spread awareness of this and change the world back to normal before the Time-Correction-Squares consumed everything back to the dawn of time and erased all memories of the normal world.

This isn't just about fish roaming above us anymore, it's much, much more than that.

And whatever we do now with this time machine, may decide whether we make everything normal again, or break time for good."

Everyone was completely speechless after what they had just heard as they tried to comprehend everything that was just casually mentioned just then.

"Wow, that's a lot to think about," said Ben.

"Yeah, well that's just the gist of it. I explained it to you, Tom and Adam a while ago in the above, but none of you really listened," said Seth.

"Na, I listened," said Tom.

"Why are you guys looking at me as if I blew your mind right now?" asked Seth.

"Because you kind of did. That's just the gist of it? Seriously? How much further could you explain it?" asked Amanda.

"Well, I don't think we have time to discuss it in full detail because we have to get out of here soon. But I think I should mention that I don't know how far back in time the Time-Correction-Squares have gone, and that we need to stay away from them."

While they were discussing plans of what they were going to do next, the city behind them was experiencing the full power of the Time-Correction-Squares. Buildings were getting completely covered. Everyone and everything was smothered in them. Then as buildings started to crumble into glowing cubic blocks, everyone in the group had worked out exactly what they were going to do next. The city behind them had crumbled into the ground with everything else as the Time-Correction-Squares spread across the fields and houses behind them.

Then as everyone stood in a close circle and Ben pushed the red button, they all started to spin in blurs of light. Then Tom touched the time machine and made it travel with them. The Time-Correction-Squares were spreading even closer to them and just before it reached the group, they vanished into the vortex, gone from reality to enter a different place in time.

As they flew through the vortex, up ahead the side of it opened up and something came out of it to head in the same direction as the others. The side of the vortex closed up, but everyone that saw the thing appear, thought they just imagined. That was when they flew into the bright light and blacked out.

The Time-Correction-Squares spread past them as they vanished, and continued to spread further and further.

Speeding up and impossible to stop. It continued in many different places across the world, spreading over everything, resetting time to ensure that sea life continue to rule The World Above, and air life continued to suffer in The World Below.

The World Above
New Frontier
Chapter 36
Interrogation

Back in the World Above, an interrogation had commenced.
"What is so special about this human anyway? I mean, it's a
science experiment gone wrong," said the curious fish.
"Yes, but how did this human become like this? What
technology do they have to enable this creature to be created?"
asked another fish.
"Bad technology, that's what it is," smirked a third fish.
"You idiot, this human has been combined with some kind of
human toy. If they had the power to combine things, we need
to work out how."
"I guess, but we're not going to get any information out of this
abomination to nature since it probably can't even understand
us right now."

As the two fish were talking, Harry continued to sit in the
glass container, alone. He didn't know what would happen to
him. Would they experiment on him? Torture him? Eat him?
He had no idea and was becoming a little worried.

As Harry sat there quietly, he soon started to shiver. Then a
dark greenish fog appeared around him. The greenish fog
started to circle him and get absorbed into him. Harry
immediately stood up trying to get the green fog away from
him, but it spread up his body, surrounding him. The fish
noticed Harry freaking out, but they weren't sure why because
they couldn't see the green fog. The fog was causing great

pain to Harry as he ran around in a circle and pushed himself against the glass trying to escape.

Then as the fog covered his face, the fish noticed Harry's eyes turn backwards in his head as his teeth grew pointy. Then as Harry stood up straight showing a toothy grin, the fish stared at him in confusion as to what had happened. As Harry walked back, he scratched words into the glass. The fish watched him carve these words, noticing the same word get engraved constantly. The word being repeated was saying, LOOPED, LOOPED, LOOPED. Then he collapsed to the ground shivering and exhausted.

The fish weren't sure what to think of this until Harry stood up again and spoke to the fish saying, "Ahh, finally. I'm alone again in my skin."
The fish instantly stood back in fear and utter surprise as Harry spoke to them since that was meant to be impossible. Humans didn't even seem to be able to talk to each other since they never made any noises in any condition or environment. But this human was making sounds, and somehow creating words the fish could understand.

"How are you speaking to us right now human?"
"Well, I think people used to call me Harry so you'll call me that instead of what I'm not."
"Um, you still haven't answered my question yet. How are you talking to us?"
"The experiment that changed part of me into a plastic fish caused it."
"What. But that's not possible," said the astounded fish.
"It is now, and that's not all."
"What do you mean, that's not all."

"Do you like the world you live in right now fish?"

"Um, yeah sure. I guess it's okay. Why?"

"The evil humans want your world as their world," said Harry.

"Huh!"

"You heard me, there are plans for a human invasion on your world, and if they succeed, you will be treated and hunted down, the same way you hunt humans."

"No, that can't be, humans are small and can't walk in our world."

"But they can, can't they. Look at me!"

"Mhmm."

"Look, I hate all aspects of air life. I'm even willing to help you all fight back against the evil humans, and I'm prepared to tell you everything I know about their plans. This includes the weapons they plan on using. How they're making the weapons. And how they worked out fish could get poisoned when consuming humans who'd already eaten some rubbish in the ocean.

That's right. The rubbish in the ocean has been utilised by humans to poison and kill all sea life who consume them. They're even using human trawling boats to distribute their poisoned bodies across the world!" Harry yelled.

The fish were amazed by this, and they didn't think things could get any crazier until Harry said one other thing.

"Oh and by the way, we are all in a massive time loop, and I'm going to tell you how we can stop it.

"How?"

Harry took a deep breath and said slowly, "By having a war… A war for The World Above.

The World Above
New Frontier
Epilogue

Back in the vortex, I heard one of the blue being's yell,
"Quick, send Nick into the vortex before it's too late!"
I threw Nick into the vortex after listening to what the blue
being said and watched it close behind him. Then immediately
I signalled the other two to follow me through the vortex as
the void continued to seep into it. Jacob, Scott and Teresa
were still contained with us as we glided through the time
stream and exited through the bright light, hoping Nick made
it back to the others before it was too late.

The three of us reappeared in a swampy area as planned and
we started to trudge through the muck looking for Jabnmine,
the one who started it all. Jabnmine was entirely made up of
vines and mud. It had the power to manipulate the minds of
anyone into doing whatever it wanted them to do and think.
He teleported everyone who was about to die and sent them to
a different point in time.
He was the one who froze time right when it was necessary
for every character in the World Above.
He was the one who planned everything, including the loop.
And we were here to help continue it.

As we trudged through the swamp, I noticed vines and trees
moving around everywhere. Then the ground started to move
from beneath us as the vines were getting pulled in a straight
line and gradually lifting into the air. A gust of wind flew
through the entire area as trees around us started to get pulled
into the ground. Then as I prepared to step back, not knowing

where Jabnmine would appear, the wind started to make sounds resembling a ferocious roar surrounding all of us.

Then a dark mist emerged around me as we all started to release Jacob, Scott and Teresa. The dark mist was mainly spreading up the other two beings that had been turned into the same thing I was. Then spinning circles appeared around the two beings as the dark mist continued to surround them. Jacob, Teresa and Scott had fully appeared in front of me as they started to look around in confusion and disbelief. Then Scott was the first to notice the vines stretching up his body and over his arms. Jacob tried to move away, but the vines had been wrapped around his ankles and wrists really tightly while Teresa experienced the same thing Scott was.

Then as I turned back to see the other blue beings, I watched one of them disappear with a grin on its face, while the other one disappeared into the darkness, surrounding and smothering Scott until it disappeared into him, causing him to turn limp. When the dark mist disappeared, the wind started to roar even louder as the vines wrapped around Scott's face. The spirit within him caused him to grow into a forty-year-old adult as the vines kept him still. Jacob continued to try and wriggle free, but it was no use.

Then as he looked to his side, the vines had already begun to slide into Teresa's mouth and under her skin. Then the vines started to stretch up Jacobs' legs and across his body as well. I didn't know how to feel about this as it felt like I'd seen this happen heaps of times before, but I'd never even known what was going to happen when I bought them here. Jabnmine didn't even seem to show any empathy for any of them.

The spirit seemed to be redesigning Scott to make him into a completely different person. Then Jabnmine started to whisper something to him.

"When your job is done, you must leave without being revealed, only to leave the mortals confused about the decisions made, hoping it could all be concealed."

And as that was said, Scott vanished into a blue blur with a dark mist following behind it.

The vines continued to spread across Jacobs' arms as I watched it continue over his head as Scott's brain had been completely redesigned. Teresa was shaking all over as the vines had fully covered her body and started to redesign her brain completely.

Jacob continued to move around as much as he could when he finally managed to break free and turn his head to look at me as I looked at his face of distress, not knowing what to do. He was important for the loop to continue. This had to happen. I was made so that I couldn't feel emotions. These were just orders Jabnmine gave me. Then it occurred to me. I may have been redesigned just like Scott was. I might have felt emotions once. It was too late for Teresa as the vines started to slide out of her, but as I watched the vines force open Jacobs mouth, I lifted up my arms and tried to absorb him back into me just before the vines entered.

The wind roared around me crazier than before as I had completely absorbed Jacob into me. A vine immediately shot up and wrapped itself around my wrist. Then another one shot up and got my other wrist. Then the vines started to spread up my legs. I used all the power I had left to quickly open up a vortex and managed to send Jacob into it to set him free and see the others again. As the vines spread all over me, I was prepared for the worst as I noticed spinning circles appear around Scott until he vanished into a blue light. Then soon afterwards, Teresa vanished as well.

The vines continued to spread across my face as it did something unexpected. The vines slid into my mouth and continued to slide through my skin to soon enter my brain. The pain was unimaginable, but I had no way of showing it. It didn't matter though; I was a freak. Anything I was to become after this would be an improvement. Then as the vines finished their work on my head, they left my mouth.

I didn't feel any different as I still felt very powerful. Then I noticed the blue circles spinning around me as I tried to remember what had happened just before. I didn't even feel any different as I was still dark shaded and misty. Then as the blue circles spun faster around me, I vanished from the swamp as it was beginning to calm down again. As I fell through the vortex, I looked up ahead and noticed a bright light in front of me and fell into it.

I reappeared in the new world not knowing where or when I was, until I realised I was in a pale room. I looked monstrous as I started to spread darkness over the entire area. Then I noticed a small person in front of me trying to back away from the darkness. I tried to stop it, but everything I did made me look even more monstrous. Then as the darkness spread over the person, he got absorbed into me and I blacked out. I looked around, realising I had no control over this person's body. The person then started to walk around on all fours when I realised the guy wasn't a person anymore, he was a mere house pet. A cat.

Jabnmine must have planned all of this. I had to be disguised as something sneaky to tag along with Ben and Tom. Then as I watched them argue about who got to drive to the pier, I ran around the car until Tom picked me up and placed me in the house. The loop was continuing all over again and I needed to go with them. So I managed to sneak out of the house and run under the car to hide.

Then as I felt the earthquake shake the ground and crack some windows, I knew it had begun again, and I had to turn human to communicate to the others. Somehow I had to find a way to stop it before everything looped again.

And then, I completely forgot everything. My mind went blank. I didn't know about Jabnmine, what was going to happen to the world, nothing. All I knew was that I had to tag along with my owner and his brother, mainly because they were going on a fishing trip and I was probably going to get some fish guts to eat afterwards. But when the earthquake that scared me away from the car finished, I realised that there could've been another reason why I wanted to go with them. I just wasn't sure why yet, so I snuck into the car and hid under the blankets without anyone realising. Ready, for the fishing trip to begin.

About the Author:

Ben Gorry, the author of 'The World Above, New Frontier,' lives with his brother Tom, and parents Russell and Corinne. He is 18 years old and studies year 12 VCE in school.

Ben has been writing books since he was 8 years old and is also the author of, 'The Curse of the Slimy Green Monster,' and 'The World Above'.

He has achieved an adult Black Belt in Taekwondo and is also a competent snow skier, tacking black runs with confidence.

Ben aspires to continue writing books and hopes that they could eventually become blockbuster movies.

www.ingramcontent.com/pod-product-compliance
Lightning Source LLC
Chambersburg PA
CBHW060551260626
47161CB00003B/1147